In our wet suits, we flutter-kicked our way through the dark ocean. Wirenut first, me second, and TL brought up the rear.

Water plugged my ears, permitting me to hear only my heartbeat and slow deep breaths.

Through my night goggles, I kept my vision focused on Wirenut's fins. *One misstep rigs the mansion to explode.*

Talk about pressure.

We made it through the fence and continued underwater around the island to the east side.

We exited the water and stripped our diving gear, then piled it on the sliver of rocky beach.

From his vest, Wirenut pulled four pressurized suction cups. Two he strapped to his knees and two he held in his hands. TL and I did the same. Air release controlled the suction, allowing for silent attachment and release. They worked on any surface.

Wirenut turned to us, touched his eye, and held up one finger. *Watch closely. One at a time.*

TL and I nodded. Wirenut suctioned onto the stone and began a spiderlike crawl. I scrutinized his form, memorizing his technique and rhythm.

He made it to the roof and signaled for me.

One misstep rigs the mansion to explode.

With a deep breath I suctioned onto the wall.

other books you may enjoy

the specialists
down to the wire

shannon greenland

speak

An Imprint of Penguin Group (USA) Inc.

SPEAK

Published by the Penguin Group

Penguin Group (USA) Inc., 345 Hudson Street, New York, New York 10014, U.S.A.

Penguin Group (Canada), 90 Eglinton Avenue East, Suite 700,

Toronto, Ontario, Canada M4P 2Y3 (a division of Pearson Penguin Canada Inc.)

Penguin Books Ltd, 80 Strand, London WC2R 0RL, England

Penguin Ireland, 25 St Stephen's Green, Dublin 2, Ireland

(a division of Penguin Books Ltd)

Penguin Group (Australia), 250 Camberwell Road, Camberwell, Victoria 3124, Australia

(a division of Pearson Australia Group Pty Ltd)

Penguin Books India Pvt Ltd, 11 Community Centre,

Panchsheel Park, New Delhi - 110 017, India

Penguin Group (NZ), 67 Apollo Drive, Rosedale, North Shore 0745, Auckland, New Zealand

(a division of Pearson New Zealand Ltd.)

Penguin Books (South Africa) (Pty) Ltd, 24 Sturdee Avenue,

Rosebank, Johannesburg 2196, South Africa

Registered Offices: Penguin Books Ltd, 80 Strand, London WC2R 0RL, England

Published by Speak, an imprint of Penguin Group (USA) Inc., 2007

10 9 8 7 6 5 4 3 2 1

LIBRARY OF CONGRESS CATALOGING-IN-PUBLICATION DATA

Greenland, Shannon.

The specialists : down to the wire / by Shannon Greenland.

p. cm.

Summary: GiGi, a sixteen-year-old computer genius living undercover with a group of teen-aged prodigies, goes on a mission with Wirenut, the electronics specialist, when a deadly neurotoxin is stolen and hidden in a small Mediterranean country.

[1. Espionage—Fiction. 2. Orphans—Fiction.] I. Title. II. Title: Down to the wire.

PZ7.G8458Sod 2007

[Fic]—dc22 2006102666

Speak ISBN 978-0-14-240917-6

Printed in the United States of America

ACKNOWLEDGMENTS

Thanks to all the girls who gave their critiquing brilliance: Glen McGafferty, Tara Greenbaum, Mari Lacroix, and Courtney Nighbert.

Tons of hoorays for my fab plotting group: Shelly Gilchrist, Tara Greenbaum, and Britta Harris.

A toast to you, Nadia Cornier, for being the coolest agent ever.

And one for you, too, Karen Chaplin. You are, hands down, the dream editor.

To all my young adult friends at Teen Lit Authors, you gals are the best group.

And to all my family in alphabetical order, so none of them will complain I've left them out: Bill, Jason, Jim, Mark, Max, Melinda, Naomi, Sharie, and Susan. Thanks for being the best support group a gal could ask for.

▓[proloque]

using his homemade. handheld computer, the HOMAS B28, Frankie flipped through prescanned floor plans.

Impenetrable. That's what all the suppliers, media, and tech journals were bragging about the Rayver Security System.

We'll just see about that.

He tucked the B28 in his zippered thigh pocket and pulled out a granola bar.

Unwrapping it, Frankie studied the dark New Mexico Museum of History from the sidewalk. Easy enough to get in the front door. Standard nixpho lock with a keypad. Any kindergartener with half an IQ could do it, too.

He folded the chewy bar in half and shoved the whole thing in his mouth. Apple cinnamon. Not his favorite, but it was all the corner store had.

The true challenge of this job lay in the triple-sealed, flex-steel vault. Protected by the oh-so-impressive Rayver Security System.

Frankie didn't know what was in the vault. Didn't care. He was here to crack the impenetrable Rayver System. No more, no less. Just to prove he could do it.

Tossing the wrapper in the already full garbage can, he crossed the shadowed street.

The two-story brick museum stood at the end of a long dead-end road with woods along the back and sides.

It was deserted. Too good to be true.

Frankie pulled his hood down over his face as he neared the entrance.

Five-five-six-four-three-zero. He punched in the code he'd seen the museum manager use every night this week. Anybody with binoculars and enough patience could've retrieved it, too.

Click. The door unlocked, and he slipped inside.

Standing in the entranceway, he scanned the dimly lit interior, recalling the layout. Left. Two rooms. Stairwell down. One room to the right.

"Okay, Frankie," he whispered to himself. "Game's on. Don't get too confident. Never know what might happen."

He closed his eyes and blew out a long slow breath. Then, with quiet feet, he shuffled left into the African Bone Room. A glass display case ran the center's length.

With his back to the west wall, he watched the corner camera. From his last visit to the museum, he recalled that it scanned in two-second intervals, moving a fraction of an inch to the right with each scan. He needed to make it across the room before it scanned back. No problem.

Staying in its blind spot, Frankie baby-stepped on each two-second interval and made it safely to the other side.

He entered the New Zealand Hat Room. No display cases here.

No cameras either. Strange-looking hats hung on the walls, each rigged with an alarm should one be removed.

He squashed the mischievous urge to take one down just to prove it could be done and crossed the carpet to the stairwell on the other side.

Suddenly, he stopped in midstep. Cold prickles crawled across his skin. *Somebody's in here.*

Slowly, he pivoted, searching every corner, shadow, and inch of space.

Nothing.

A good solid minute ticked by as he listened closely. Soft air-conditioner hum. Nearly inaudible camera ticks. Quiet laser alarm buzz.

Nothing else. No shuffle of a person's feet. No breath.

Funky imagination. That's all. Although he really didn't believe himself.

From his vest pocket Frankie pulled out a wad of homemade gray putty and a six-inch length of bamboo that he used as a blowgun. Balling the putty, he fit it in the end of the bamboo.

The stairwell's camera hung catty-corner near the bottom. He rolled his black hood above his lips. Sighted down the length of the bamboo. Took a breath. Put it in his mouth. And blew.

The putty flew like a dart and plunked right on the lens.

Yeah, that's what I'm talking about.

He tiptoed down the stairs and hung a right, and his pulse jumped like it did every time a new security system challenged him.

The impenetrable Rayver System.

Impenetrable, his big toe.

He pulled down his fiber-lit goggles used for laser detection from on top of his head and fit them over his eyes.

Bingo.

Yellow lasers zigzagged the room preceding the vault. One-twothreefourfivesix . . . twenty ankle high. The same at the waist. Six on the ceiling.

Child's play. Except for the yellow, skin-sizzling color. Whatever happened to the reliable red set-off-the-alarm-but-don't-fry-the-burglar color?

Leaning to the left at a seventy-degree angle, he spied a tunnel-like opening void of lasers. *You'd think the tech geniuses would've figured this out by now.*

Frankie unbuttoned a pocket in his cargo pants and pulled out the remote-control expander. Pointing it toward the opening of the tunnel, he pressed the expander button.

A skinny metal wire snaked out, becoming stiff as it left the remote control.

Steady, Frankie, steady.

One slight movement and the wire would collapse into the lasers.

It made it through the small tunnel void of lasers, across the room, and straight into the tiny hole below the vault's lock.

The lasers flicked off, and he quickly set his watch. He had exactly one minute and seventeen seconds until they turned back on.

Reeling in the expandable wire, he ran over the open tile to the vault. He yanked a tool kit from his vest and laid the triple-folded leather pouch on the ground. He took nitrox, a metal adhesive release, and squirted the control panel.

It popped off, and Frankie caught it before it clanged to the ground. Anything over twenty-five decibels would set off the alarm.

Multicolored wires crisscrossed and tangled with one another.

A diversion.

He reached in, grabbed the clump, and ripped them right out. Red lasers immediately flicked on, filling the control panel opening.

Frankie took the extra-long needle-nose wire cutters from his tool pouch and, leaning to the left at a seventy-degree angle, found his opening.

Carefully, he inserted the wire cutters through the opening surrounded by lasers and snipped the one remaining white wire at the very back.

The vault clicked open. The control panel lasers flicked off. Frankie checked his watch.

Twenty seconds remaining.

Snatching up the tools, he flung the vault door open. A small wooden man, an artifact of some sort, sat on a stand in the middle of the vault.

A weight-sensitive stand.

Crud.

He hadn't expected that.

Frankie estimated the artifact at three pounds and took three one-pound pellets from his tool pouch. Holding his breath, he slipped the artifact off and the pellets on all in one smooth motion.

And froze.

Nothing. Only silence.

No alarms. No lasers.

He checked his watch.

Three seconds remaining.

Frankie sprinted back across the room. His watch alarm dinged. He dove the last few feet and whipped around to see the yellow lasers flick back on.

Whew.

Smiling, he did his victory shoulder-roll dance.

Oh, yeah. Frankie got it going on.

Go, Frankie. Go, Frankie. Go. Go.

He packed his stuff, slipped a yellow ribbon from his sock, and tied it around the artifact. It was his signature. He wished he could be here to see them discover it outside its *impenetrable* vault.

With a pat to its head, he stood.

"Cute," a voice spoke.

Frankie spun around. Another person stood behind him.

Pointing a gun.

His heart stopped. Then he saw the gun shake.

Why…he's nervous.

The other guy flicked it toward the artifact. "Give it to me." Something distorted his voice.

Frankie ran his gaze down the length of the other burglar and back up. He looked like a skinnier version of Frankie. Black cargo pants and vest. Black hood. Black martial arts slippers.

"I said, Give it to me."

Frankie shrugged. "Sure." Why did he care? He hadn't come for this silly thing anyway.

Behind the hood, the burglar narrowed his eyes, like he didn't believe it'd be that easy.

"It's all yours." Frankie stepped to the side.

The burglar paused. Shook his head. "Hand it to me."

Frankie sighed. "Oh, all right." He snatched it from the ground and tossed it to the burglar.

The burglar's eyes widened as he fumbled with the gun and caught the artifact.

Frankie watched him juggle the two things. He could totally take down this idiot. The burglar was *way* too amusing, though, and Frankie needed a good laugh.

Holding the artifact to his chest, the burglar scrambled to get the gun pointed back at Frankie. "You think you're funny, don't you?"

He shrugged. Yeah, actually, he did.

The burglar backed his way up the stairs, still pointing the gun at Frankie.

"Can't fire that thing, ya know. You'll set off the alarms in this place."

The burglar paused in his backward ascent as if he hadn't thought about that. "You're the Ghost, aren't you?"

Frankie gave his best sixteenth-century bow. "The one and only."

"I . . . I've studied you."

The small admission pumped his ego. "Then you know I'm no threat. I did what I came here to do."

Seconds ticked by. The burglar slipped the gun inside his vest.

"Safety," Frankie reminded him.

"It's not loaded."

He laughed at having been tricked.

The burglar raced up the stairs toward the New Zealand Hat Room, and Frankie followed. With his back to the west wall, the burglar inched around the African Bone Room.

Frankie watched his fluid, timed movements as he kept pace with the camera that scanned in two-second intervals. Not such a novice. He'd been trained.

"Who are you?" Frankie whispered across both rooms.

The other burglar stopped and looked back.

"Keep moving!" Frankie hissed at the exact second the burglar missed his two-second step and set off the alarm.

Crud.

The burglar bolted from the room and up the steps to the second floor.

Frankie raced after him, through a narrow hallway and into a huge room. Then he disappeared behind the door to a janitor closet.

Staying right on his heels, Frankie flung open the closet door. The burglar snaked up a rope hanging fifteen feet from an open skylight.

Quick guy.

He'd rigged the skylight alarm with an eraser, a small piece of aluminum foil, and, although Frankie couldn't see it, he knew a dab of olive oil. That particular combination of three elements shorted out standard valumegal wiring. He'd introduced that five years ago, and criminals had copied it ever since.

Sirens filtered through the air, and his pulse jumped. Cops. About a quarter of a mile away.

Yeah, baby, thrill of the chase.

The burglar made it to the roof, and Frankie started his ascent. Halfway there he looked up to see the burglar holding a knife to the rope.

No.

"Sorry," the burglar mumbled, and sliced it clean.

Son of a— Frankie fell and landed on his back. "Umph."

Footsteps pounded outside the door. He jumped to his feet and leapt for the skylight.

The door flew open. "Hold it right there."

Frankie froze and squeezed his eyes shut.

Crud. Double crud.

"Put your hands up."

He stuck his hands in the air. *I'm going to prison for this.*

"Now turn around. *Real* slow."

Opening his eyes, Frankie pivoted.

Someone yanked off his hood and shined a light in his face. Frankie squinted.

"Well, look here. You're just a kid." The cop jerked Frankie's arms back and handcuffed him. "You have the right to remain silent. . . ." The cop hauled Frankie through the museum and out the door.

As the cop shoved Frankie in the squad car, Frankie glanced toward the woods. The burglar stood in the shadows, watching.

░ ░ ░

Frankie sat at a table in an interrogation room. He'd been there for hours.

"Where is it?" The red-faced, big-gut cop slammed his fist on the table.

For the trillionth time.

It scared Frankie the first, say, two times he did it. Now it just annoyed him. "I don't have it," he repeated. "The other guy took it."

The cop clinched his jaw so hard it made his puffy cheeks vibrate.

Calm down, man. You're gonna have a heart attack.

"Nice *ballet slippers*, fancy boy."

For your information, these are handmade, double-layered martial arts slippers. The outer coating slick for sliding. Peel away to the rubber underneath for climbing.

Frankie's stomach growled loudly. "Can I please have something to eat?" They didn't understand. His metabolism ate calories fast. If he didn't get something soon, he'd get the shakes.

"Eat?" the cop growled. "Are you kidding me? Tell me where the artifact is, and I'll personally shove a burger down your throat."

"Thanks, *buddy*, but no. However inviting that burger sounds." Smart-ass remark. But the cop deserved it.

The cop's entire body shook in response.

I'm really pissing this guy off. "Listen, take some breaths. You're about to pop an artery." Although that'd be mildly satisfying to watch.

The cop reared back and shoved Frankie in the chest, and he flew out of the metal chair.

The interrogation room door clicked open and a guy in a brown suit walked in. He looked at the heavy-breathing, shaking, red-faced cop, then turned calm eyes on Frankie. "Come with me."

Flipping the cop off in his mind, Frankie pushed up from his sprawled position on the floor. He followed the guy through the police station and out the front doors into a hot, dry New Mexico morning. Not a single cop tried to stop them.

The guy led Frankie to a black SUV with tinted windows.

Opening the back door, the guy nodded Frankie inside.

What was going on? Something didn't feel right. Serial killers abducted people this way.

Frankie glanced back at the police station. No one had stopped them. This guy must be legit.

The guy reached inside his jacket and pulled out a wallet. He flipped it open. "Thomas Liba. IPNC."

IPNC?

Frankie studied the man's identification. Same light brown skin. Weird green eyes. Curly brown hair.

Frankie peeked inside the vehicle. It looked more like a cargo van than an SUV. Two benches faced each other, and locked cabinets lined the walls.

With one last look at Thomas, Frankie stepped up into the SUV and got the odd sensation his whole life was about to change.

Thomas closed the door. He opened a wall-mounted fuse box, pressed a button, and air-conditioning began to flow through the vents.

Taking the seat across from Frankie, Thomas pointed to a cooler under Frankie's bench. "Help yourself."

Food! He dove in. Sandwiches, sodas, cookies, chips, fruit, carrot sticks. Oh yeah, a starving man's paradise.

Thomas opened a folder. "Francisco Badaduchi."

Yep. That'd be me. He swallowed. *Love* ham and cheese. "I go by Frankie."

Thomas nodded. "Italian American. Five feet ten. One

hundred and seventy pounds. Seventeen years old. One hundred fifty IQ. Black hair. Dark brown eyes. Goatee. Thorn tattoo around your upper arm." He tapped his folder. "You've got quite a record. Mostly five-finger discount. Seems a bit beneath your skills."

Beneath my skills? How would he know that?

Frankie popped a cookie in his mouth. "See something I want, I help myself to it." Anything to get arrested.

"Like juvy hall better than the boys' home, I take it."

Frankie stopped chewing. He stared across the SUV at Thomas, a hunk of cookie in his mouth. *How'd he know that?*

"I was like you once. A system kid. Hated the boys' home. Hated what they did to me there. Juvy hall's safer. Patrolled. I know."

Forcing the unchewed cookie down his throat, Frankie closed the cooler. Food didn't seem so interesting anymore.

Thomas consulted his file again. "Your uncle's on death row for—"

"What do you want with me?" Buried panic tightened Frankie's gut.

"You have a scar on your upper left shoulder where he—"

"What do you want with me?" Memories Frankie did *not* intend to relive.

"Okay. We don't have to talk about your past." Thomas closed the file. "According to court psychologists, you are highly intelligent and handle yourself with humor. You have the potential to be dangerous because of what you witnessed as a child. No one wanted to adopt you because they were afraid of your mental stability."

Idiots. All of them. What did they know anyway? "I said, what do you want with me?"

"I know you're the Ghost. I've followed your career since your first breaking and entering at ten years old."

"I don't know what you're talking about." Bluffer. No way he had evidence. Frankie was too good.

"No more juvy hall. You're going to prison. For a long time. No escape. Know what they do to guys like you in there?"

Frankie swallowed, trying not to be intimidated. "I've heard."

"Then you know it's a place you don't want to be." Thomas opened his file again and flipped through some pages. "You've got quite an online fan club. They buy your homemade electronic contraptions and keep you in business."

Crud. This guy did know a lot about him.

"Fictitious accounts. Rerouted IP addresses. Clever. You've cracked the most secure systems in the world. Systems the highest trained agents haven't even broken."

It came naturally for Frankie. What could he say? "Listen, it's obvious you have my whole life right there in that handy-dandy file. So why don't you tell me what you want?"

Thomas looked up from the folder. "I want you to come work for me."

1

In her skin-tight JUST TRY ME! T-shirt, Bruiser boinged onto her bed. Her red braids boinged with her. "I love a good soap opera. I think it's so cool you two are getting a groove on." She bounced off her bed.

"Shhh." I glanced from my bed toward the open door. Now that I'd managed to convince David I wasn't his "little sister," I didn't want him to know I'd told Bruiser that I liked him. "And we're not getting a groove on." As a matter of fact, it seemed like we rarely had a moment alone.

Laughing, David entered our room, and my stomach swooshed to my feet. Please tell me he didn't just hear us.

He pointed at Bruiser. "I heard that."

Groan.

"You're more trouble than you're worth." He lifted her up in a fireman's hold and tossed her back onto her bed.

She rolled over, grinning. "But don't you all just looove me?"

Over the four and a half months I'd been with the Specialists, Bruiser's silliness hadn't changed at all. It was hard to believe that tiny freckled Molly, or Bruiser, as she'd been code-named, was our resident martial artist. At fifteen, she was a year or two younger than the rest of us. Except David—he was eighteen. But she could outlast all of us. She was a real-life version of the Energizer Bunny.

David threw a pillow at her. "We tolerate you, squirt."

He stretched out beside me on my twin-size bed, and my heart skipped a beat. His cologne swirled up my nose, and I resisted the urge to roll over and bury my face in his neck. Whatever kind he wore, I planned to buy him a whole case of it.

Wirenut strolled in. "Oh, GiGi. Brilliant, klutzy, drop-dead gorgeous GiGi. Ya know, David, you're killing all chances I could've had with this tall blondie. But that's all right. It's all good."

My face warmed at his flirting. I didn't like Frankie, aka Wirenut, our resident electronics expert, in *that* way. He was like a brother or a really cool cousin.

I glanced at him, and he winked, and I knew he was purposefully messing with me.

Wait a minute. Did he just say David killed all his chances? So Wirenut knew I liked David, too?

David stacked his hands beneath his head, and his hip brushed mine, sending a warm wave through my body. Of course Wirenut knew I liked David. Everybody probably knew. How could they not with the fumbling fool I made of myself every time I was around him?

Beaker came out of the bathroom. She snagged her chemistry book off her bed and slid down in her corner of the girls' dormitory room. She stuck her nose in her book and started reading.

Beaker, whose real name was Sissy, didn't seem to like anybody. Me especially. I didn't know what the problem was. I tried not to take her moods personally, but I wished she'd snap out of it. She seemed to get more and more distant as the months went by, when all the rest of us were becoming a family.

Wirenut jumped over Beaker's bed and came down next to her. He put her in a headlock and knuckle-rubbed her choppy blue hair. She pushed him away, grumbling to hide her giggle.

He pushed her back, smiling. Wirenut was the only one who could make her halfway laugh.

Who would've guessed Beaker, the Goth girl with a nose ring and dog collar, would be one of the most brilliant chemists in the world? Looks were *definitely* deceiving, as this group had proven.

"Now, now. Let's all be at peace." Mystic walked in with Parrot and parked it right in the center of the carpeted floor. He folded up his legs and touched his thumbs to his middle fingers, assuming his in-touch-with-the-world position.

Mystic, or Joe, as his real name was, had a NFL player's body, but he possessed the unique gift of clairvoyance. For some reason I never imagined a psychic would be so muscular.

Parrot sprawled across the foot of Bruiser's bed. Darren, aka Parrot, was our linguist. Sixteen languages to be exact. "Almost time for our weekly conference."

Wirenut pointed to a banana on top of my dresser. "Gonna eat that?"

"We just had burgers. You're seriously hungry?"

"Serious."

Wirenut was always eating. He should be like three hundred pounds with all the food he put away. But he just burned it all off like it was nothing. I reached over and tossed him the banana.

David's watch alarm went off. "It's time. Let's go."

We all made our way from our room, past the guys' room and TL's office, and down the long hallway to the elevator.

David placed his hand on the globe light fixture. The hidden laser scanned his print pattern, then the mountainous wall mural slid open to reveal the secret elevator. We all crammed into the small space. David punched in his personal code, and the elevator descended four floors beneath the California ranch where we lived.

We filed out and down the underground hallway, past all the locked doors, including mine and Chapling's computer lab, and came to a stop at the conference room. Thomas Liba, TL, our team leader, sat at the head of a long metal table studying a file. Erin and Adam from Specialists Team One sat to TL's left.

Rolling out the black leather chairs, we took our seats around the table, with David sitting in his usual spot to TL's right.

TL leaned over and whispered something in David's ear, and he nodded. David was TL's right-hand guy. David had lived here his whole life, longer than anybody else. The ranch used to be a safe house for the children of the nation's top agents. With his father being an agent, David grew up here. Now he was being trained to be a strategist, just like TL.

TL stood. "Afternoon, everybody."

We all greeted him.

He closed the file in front of him. "This'll be a quick meeting, as I have a prospective client to meet with. I want to begin by saying that this has been a productive week. We've been a private organization for a month now, and it has opened all sorts of avenues."

With a contained grin, Bruiser nudged me. "Go, GiGi," she mumbled.

I smiled. I'd found the funding that allowed the Specialists to break away from the government and become private.

"As you can tell"—TL motioned around the room—"Piper, Tina, and Curtis from Team One are not here. The girls are in Australia, and Curtis is in Japan. The money we'll make from those two missions alone should sustain us for the next three years. So"—he nodded—"as I said, this had been a productive week."

Everyone applauded.

TL held up his hand for quiet. "Everyone met Mr. Share, David's father, after the last mission to Ushbania. The mission that GiGi went on, and a successful one at that. We were all very proud of her performance on her first mission."

Bruiser nudged me again.

"After being kidnapped by a terrorist cell and held hostage for the past ten years," TL continued, "there was a lot up in the air about Mr. Share. I'm happy to say he's been cleared and is settled in his new life with his new identity."

I glanced at David, wondering when he'd be able to see his

father again. I'd have to remember to ask him later on.

"Erin," TL motioned across the table, "give us a quick update on what you and Adam are doing."

Erin rolled her eyes. "That guy who hired us to track his son is wasting his money. All the kid does is go to classes, the library, and the cafeteria."

Adam laughed. "It's too easy a job. I keep waiting for the real fun to kick in."

David smiled. "We're getting paid good money, though, to play private eye. So grin and bear it."

"Easy for you to say," Erin grumbled. "You're not the one yawning on the job."

David chuckled at that. "Speaking of job. How are you tracking him right now?"

Adam held up his watch. "Good ole GPS. We planted a bug on him."

"All right, moving on." TL propped his fingers on the table. "Everyone's report cards came in from the university and San Belden High. With the exception of Mystic's D in gym, we have all A's and B's."

Everyone looked at Mystic, and he shrugged.

"That's it for me. As I said, this would be quick." TL picked up his folder. "Questions?"

We all shook our heads.

"Dismissed." TL motioned to David, and the two of them filed out.

the next day I stood with Chapling in our computer lab, staring at his computer.

He rubbed his hands together, looking like a little boy with a really cool toy. "Ready?"

I nodded.

"Computer," he commanded.

HELLO, MR. CHAPLING, the computer typed back.

He giggled. "Coolcoolcool. It worked."

I looked down at him. "Mr. Chapling?"

He shrugged, all innocent. "What? I deserve some respect." Chapling elbowed me. "Now you try."

"Computer," I commanded.

HELLO, GIGI.

"It said my nickname." I laughed. "That *is* cool."

"*It's* a she," Chapling informed me.

I held back a smile. "Of course."

"I'm so smart." He clapped. "Smartsmartsmart."

Chapling had been working on this new voice-activated system for months. And obviously, he was thrilled with the fact that it worked. But of course it would work; Chapling was a genius.

"Watch this." His eyes brightened. "Computer, give me everything on . . ." He glanced at me, and I shrugged. "Costa Rica," he said.

ONE MOMENT, PLEASE.

Chapling bounced. "I always wanted to go to Costa Rica. Thought I might try surfing."

"Surfing? You?"

He looked offended for about a second. "What? You can't see me surfing?"

I thought about that—his little, chubby, redheaded self riding a wave—and shook my head. "Nope. Can't see you surfing."

Chapling shrugged. "Yeah, well, me neither. But it's fun to think about."

Information scrolled across the computer screen, and we watched. Pictures, newspaper articles, history . . . anything a person could ever want on Costa Rica.

He did a jig. "Is she awesome or what?"

Smiling, I checked my watch. "Shoot. I'm going to be late for PT. Gotta go."

I raced from the lab, through the underground corridors, up the elevator, and down the hall into our bedroom. Quickly, I changed clothes for physical training, slipping on a sweatshirt and a pair of exercise shorts. David had bought them for me during my first few weeks on the ranch. I'd shoved them into the depths of my dresser, planning on returning them. *Guess I changed my mind.*

I zipped into the adjoining bathroom and gave my body a quick once-over in the mirror. I checked my front and sides and triple-checked my butt. You wouldn't have caught me anywhere near these shorts a few months ago. With PT, though, I'd developed some tone and felt more confident now. I used to think these shorts were too short. They weren't. Girls wore them all the time around campus.

Pulling my hair into a ponytail, I rushed across the room and out the door, straight into Bruiser.

"Hey." She grabbed my arm. "I was wondering where you were."

How sweet.

"Yowza, babe." She whistled. "You're hot."

Let's hope David thinks so, too.

She pointed to her snug long-sleeve T-shirt. YO! I'M MEAN. DO I LOOK IT? "Got it yesterday. Like?"

"Yeah, I like." Bruiser always had on a different custom-made T-shirt. "I swear, with the money you spend, you probably keep the local screen printer in business."

"Probably." She skipped down the hall. "Come on."

She'd drawn martial arts symbols on an ace bandage that was wrapped around her knee. Bruiser *always* had an injury.

"What'd you do this time?"

"I tried a triple back flip from the ranch's roof." She shrugged. "Ended up a double."

We exited the building, and I glanced up at the roof. That had to be at least twenty feet. No way I'd try anything off that, unless lots of ropes and harnesses were involved.

Bruiser had no fear.

We passed our brand-new in-ground pool, which sat beside the house. "Wanna go for a swim later?" Bruiser asked.

"Sure."

"Let's go." She raced across the yard to the barn, where our physical training was always held, and I followed. We opened the door and made our way toward Mystic, Parrot, and Beaker, who were standing off to the right near the dumbbells.

Beaker wore her usual combat boots, dog collar, and black clothes. She'd chosen green lipstick over black and changed out her nose jewelry. Instead of her ring, a chain connected her nostril to her ear.

Let's hope it doesn't get yanked out during PT.

They all glanced down at my shorts as we approached. They weren't used to seeing me in them since I usually wore yoga pants.

"Well." This from Mystic.

"Huh." That from Parrot.

"Nice chicken legs," snided Beaker.

Bruiser was always kidding me about my chicken legs, too. From her it came out totally amusing and fun. One friend teasing another.

From Beaker? Lighthearted camaraderie wasn't part of her personality.

Nice nose chain, I wanted to snide back, but didn't.

Bruiser looped her arm through mine and turned me around. She rolled her eyes to the right. "What do you think of Adam?" she whispered.

Adam from Team One stood across the barn talking to David

and Erin. David had his back to me. He didn't know I'd come in yet.

"Well," Bruiser prompted.

I surveyed Adam's messy blond hair and tall, lean body. I'd say he stood at least six feet five. Definitely the tallest person here at the ranch. "He's all right, if you like blonds."

Bruiser elbowed me. "You're a blond."

I elbowed her back.

"He's been talking to me a lot more lately. I used not to think he was cute. But now I do. Weird, huh?"

"Nah, it's not weird. He's got a great personality, and he's cute."

"I'd need a ladder to kiss him. I'm like five feet, and he's like, what, a giant?"

I busted out laughing. Leave it to Bruiser to say something like that.

David turned from his conversation. His gaze dropped to my legs and then came up to meet my eyes. My entire body shot to boiling point, and I knew my face had to be flaming red.

He didn't look away, *wouldn't* look away.

I wished I was one of those girls who could boldly hold a guy's heated stare. Honestly, I was about to be sick.

Smiling, David bounced his brows, breaking the sexually tense moment, and I released a shaky breath.

Jonathan clapped his hands, and my attention shifted from David to our PT instructor. "Everyone over here."

As we followed Jonathan's instructions, my first PT came back to me with clarity. Falling on my head. Praying I *wouldn't* be paired with David.

I'd come a long way.

We all came in closer, and I found myself standing next to Erin.

"Remember that PT a few years ago when we bumped heads and I broke my nose?" Erin said to David, nudging him with a smile.

He grimaced. "Don't remind me," he said, and playfully nudged her back.

I didn't know why, but their cuteness bothered me.

"Spread out," Jonathan graveled, knocking me from my thoughts. "Arm's length between you. Feet together. Palms to the floor."

I followed Jonathan's orders, gritting my teeth, missing the ground by more than a foot.

Okay, so maybe I *hadn't* come such a long way.

Five minutes later he split us into partners. *Please give me David. Pleasepleaseplease give me David.*

"Know what I heard?" whispered Beaker, who was standing on the other side of me.

I shook my head, listening to Jonathan pair us up.

"David and Erin used to date."

What?

"Parrot's with Adam." Jonathan pointed to Bruiser. "Bruiser and Mystic. Beaker's with GiGi. And David's with Erin."

David's with Erin?

Wait a minute. I'm with Beaker?

I glanced over at her. She narrowed her eyes ever so slightly. *What* exactly was her problem?

We each grabbed a mat and dragged them over to the corner. I glanced at Erin, sizing her up. Average height. Shoulder-length dark hair. Athletic build. She'd always been nice to me. She was the first person I met, actually, when I arrived here in San Belden.

She and David used to date? Why hadn't David told me? Did they feel anything for each other now? Did David want to get back with her? Did she want to get back with him? Was Erin jealous? Was I? I glanced at Beaker—maybe she was just messing with me. But by the look on her face, I didn't think so.

"We're practicing floor restraint today." Jonathan stepped onto a mat, interrupting my rambling thoughts. "When you're on the bottom, how to gain control of the guy on top."

Suddenly, David shot across the room, and I jumped.

He tackled Jonathan, plastering him to the floor. Wrapping both legs around David's waist, Jonathan looped their arms together and bent David's back.

Shifting, Jonathan straightened one leg and crossed the other over David's back. "Notice the position of my legs. This prevents my opponent from rolling out of the shoulder lock."

Jonathan rotated David's wrist toward his head. "Continuous pressure in this direction will dislocate my opponent's shoulder."

David and Jonathan released each other and jumped to their feet, our signal to begin the maneuver.

Beaker and I looked at each other. Her frown said she dreaded this as much as I did.

Behind me someone grunted. A body smacked to a mat. Someone else growled.

Everyone was already at it while Beaker and I continued eyeing each other.

A girl giggled. A guy laughed. Wait a minute. I knew that laugh. *David*.

I whipped around. David had his legs wrapped around Erin's waist and her arm bent back. She giggled again.

I narrowed my eyes. They were having *way* too much fun all intertwined like that.

"Aren't they cute," Beaker sneered.

I whipped back around and lunged, tackling her. She landed so hard her nose chain rattled. I couldn't quite believe I just did that.

TL stepped into the barn. "David, GiGi, Wirenut."

Beaker shoved me off her. I gave her my best don't-mess-with-me glare before turning to TL.

"Conference room." TL headed off. "Five minutes."

2

David. Wirenut. and I stepped onto the elevator.

"Why do you think TL wants to see me?" Wirenut smoothed his fingers down his trim goatee. "Food, school, physical training, homework, chores, sleep. That's been my week. I haven't done anything wrong. Did anything go wrong on the Ushbania mission? Did my schematics provide faulty information?"

Simultaneously, David and I shook our heads, hiding our amusement. Poor Wirenut. I was just as nervous the first time TL had wanted to see me away from the rest of the group. Right before he sent me on my first mission.

Which meant that Wirenut might be going on his first mission, too. But why would I be meeting with TL? It made sense David would; TL involved him in everything. But why me?

Unless he was sending me on another mission. I groaned inwardly. Whatever happened to working from home base?

"Last week I swapped chores with Mystic," Wirenut continued worriedly. "We didn't tell TL. Do you think he's pissed about that? Ya know, overriding his authority or something."

David shook his head, all calm. "No. But I wouldn't do that again."

Wirenut expelled a short burst of air. "Crud. What have I done? Since joining the Specialists, I've been living cleaner than ever before."

I linked arms with him. "Everything's going to be okay." And I truly believed that. It was one of the most important things I'd learned since being with the Specialists. TL had only our best interest in mind. He really cared about each one of us.

The elevator stopped on Subfloor Four, and we made our way past a few locked doors to the conference room where TL waited.

Wirenut rapped on the open door. "You ever gonna tell me what's behind those locked doors?"

He made stupid attempts at humor when he was nervous.

Without looking up, TL motioned us in. "When you're ready." He pointed to me and Wirenut. "You two have a seat." TL rolled his leather chair out and stood. "David, come with me."

"When I'm ready?" Wirenut asked after TL and David left. "What does that mean?" He looked at me. "You've got access to one of the doors. Apparently, *you're* ready."

TL had given me access to the government's highest-level computer lab. Although we had split from the government, we were still able to access their resources. My team knew that it was a computer lab and that Chapling worked in there, but I wasn't allowed to give them the details of what went on inside. The secretiveness of the lab was both a curse and a privilege. Right now, with Wirenut's remark, it felt more like a curse.

"When I'm ready," Wirenut mocked. "I could break into those stupid locked doors if I wanted to."

"Wirenut—"

"TL should be rewarding me for having such self-control," he railroaded on. "That in and of itself proves I'm ready. Maybe I should tell him that."

He was right. With his electronics expertise, Wirenut *could* break into anything. It was the whole reason TL recruited him. Right now, though, his stress was making him act tough and ridiculous.

"Should I speak first?" Wirenut shifted in his chair. "Ya know, break the ice. Conversation comes easy for me. Light. Fun. Nothing serious. Who wants serious? Serious sucks. Silence comes easy, too. Hey, I'm not called the Ghost for nothing."

Wirenut expelled another short burst of frustrated air. "Okay, this is officially driving me insane. Why did TL tell us five minutes if he didn't really want us here in five? I mean, it's been seven minutes. Where is he? What, he wanted to see how long it took us to get down here? What'd he think, we'd drag our feet or something? What the hell, man, I don't drag my feet around this place. If anything, I'm faster than the others on my team. Well, except for Bruiser. But come on, she's like a freak of nature."

He was rambling to himself now. This wasn't good. "How about we talk about something else," I suggested. Wirenut needed to get his brain on another topic.

He looked across the table at me, clearly expecting me to

come up with something to talk about. Oh, okay. Um . . .

Suddenly the first day we all met popped into my mind. "Do you remember the first day we all met? The six of us sat around this same table."

Wirenut smiled. "We were all scoping out one another. Curious. Wondering what our new lives would be like."

I grinned as TL and David returned. Closing the door, TL took his seat at the head of the table. He opened a file and studied it. The header, QUID PLUOLIUM, ran across each page of small typed paragraphs. "Top Secret" had been stamped in red at the bottom.

Squinting my eyes, I studied the upside-down paragraphs. But the small print and my lack of glasses kept me from making out the details. I glanced up at TL. He didn't acknowledge any of us.

Beside me, David waited patiently, his gaze calmly fixed on the windowless wall behind Wirenut.

Across from me, Wirenut tapped his finger on the table, obviously as anxious as me.

We waited in silence for what felt like hours. Nothing from TL.

"So," Wirenut finally interrupted the silence.

Without looking up, TL shook his head in response.

Wirenut tightened his jaw, and I sent him an it's-going-to-be-okay, I-know-exactly-how-you-feel look.

My impatience brought on a teeny bit of nerves, and just

when I decided to run code sequences through my brain, TL closed the file.

"Take off your monitoring patch," he said to Wirenut.

I smiled. I bet he *was* going on a mission. TL had taken my patch right before sending me to Ushbania.

With some hesitation and a reassuring nod from David, Wirenut reached beneath his T-shirt sleeve and peeled off what looked like a nicotine patch. That's what he told anybody outside the ranch who asked about it.

He gave TL the skin-colored device. "Why do you want my tracker? Did it malfunction?"

"No. You don't need it anymore."

Wirenut grinned. "Does this mean that I'm a full-fledged Specialist?"

TL chuckled. "Yes, you're a full-fledged Specialist."

I loved when TL smiled and laughed. It made me all cozy inside. He didn't do it enough. He seemed too focused and serious most of the time.

He held up the device. "Do you remember what I told you when you first put this on?"

Wirenut nodded. "Yep. You said, 'Understand that your public education is part of your training. It's socializing; learning to lie to others regarding your past, current situation, and future. Each of you will wear a detection device for monitoring. Everything you say and do will be recorded. You will wear this until I feel confident you'll do fine without it.'"

Wow. How unbelievable that he remembered every single word.

Wirenut leaned back and folded his arms, looking very full of himself. "How was that?"

TL shook his head, like he did every time he had no clue what to do with Wirenut. "Nicely done."

"Thank you very much. Feel free to applaud."

TL's lips twitched. "All right, all kidding aside. I took GiGi's device before she left on her mission to Ushbania."

Wirenut sat up. "Does this mean I'm going somewhere?"

TL held his hand up. "I'll tell you what I told her. You've proven to be adept at your cover. You've gone about your day-to-day activities smoothly, naturally, and without a second thought. You've seamlessly merged into this world. But what I'm most impressed with is that you've had a lot of temptation. Not only around here, but at school. And not once have you given in to the mischievous urges that drove the Ghost."

Wirenut grinned, obviously pleased TL recognized that.

"The old Frankie would've been sneaking around the ranch at night, trying to break into restricted areas. I know you wouldn't have stolen anything. You would've just tied a yellow ribbon and gone on your way. But the fact that you haven't tells me you're ready to move on to the next stage of your training."

Wirenut grinned again, and I could just visualize the happy dance going on inside of him.

TL stood. "Follow me."

We left the conference room and headed down the underground hallway.

As we passed Chapling's and my computer lab, TL nodded to it. "Later on this evening, GiGi will show you around her lab."

Wirenut and I exchanged surprised glances (more on my end than his). In a few hours, Chapling's and my computer lab would no longer be a secret. It sort of bummed me out. I liked having something just mine and Chapling's.

We stopped at a door ten feet from my lab. "This will be your studio," TL said to Wirenut, stepping to the side. "Do your thing."

Oooh, neat. I was about to see inside another one of the mysterious locked doors. Wirenut must be ecstatic. Okay, now I couldn't *wait* to show him the lab.

He scrutinized the steel door and then tapped it with his finger. "Four-decibel, hollow echo. Double-reinforced. Lined with . . ." He tapped it again. "Glass. Interesting. Counter-sunk hinges."

Leaning down, he studied the lock. "Triple-plated. Imbedded." He sniffed. "Copper wax. Rigged with a laser crawler."

He got down on his knees and put his ear against the door. "Bottom left quadrant. *Tsss. Tsss. Tsss.* One-second electrical surges. A dom sensor." He held out his hand. "I need my tools."

David extended a triple-folded leather pouch.

Wirenut took it from him. He closed his eyes and rubbed it between his hands. He brought it to his face and inhaled. "Old leather, oil, and metal. It's been a long time since I've held this. I never imagined I'd miss an old pouch so much."

He spread it open on the tile floor beside him. He slipped out three wrenches, some silver wire, a lighter, a stopwatch, and some electrical tape. He inserted one wrench in the lock and wedged one in the door's upper-right corner. "This last one will be taped at a sixty-two-degree angle in the lower-left quadrant."

Sixty-two-degree angle? Jeez, that's precise.

With the lighter, he soldered silver wire to each wrench, connecting the three. He touched his knuckle to the wire. "Laser crawler rhythm is *cchhh. Chch. Cchhh. Chch.*"

He pressed the stopwatch. "On the eleventh second, the door will open."

It clicked open, and my jaw dropped. Wow. Wirenut knew his stuff.

He did what he called his victory shoulder-roll dance. "Go, Wirenut. Go, Wirenut. Go. Go."

David shook his head. "We've had the best of the best test out our security."

TL slapped Wirenut on the back. "You're the first to successfully break in. Congratulations."

Wirenut's face beamed with pride. "Thanks."

I knew the feeling. Nothing felt better than pleasing TL.

David pushed open the door and turned on the light. "Get your tools and go on in."

Wirenut packed up, and we followed him in. He skidded to

a stop, and I nearly ran right into him. "That's my stuff. That's everything I've ever sold online."

All kinds of electronic contraptions lined the tables and shelves.

Wirenut shook his head. "How di— Where di— What's going on?"

TL picked up a remote control from a shelf. "You may have had ghost accounts and rerouted IPs, but I rigged it so that I was always the highest bidder when you auctioned things off."

"You mean you've been buying my contraptions for years?"

TL and David nodded.

"Man." Wirenut laughed. "That's too funny. I guess I'm not as clever as I thought."

TL pointed the remote control at the back wall, pressed a button, and the wall slid open. Wirenut sucked in a breath.

Thousands of the latest electronic devices jammed the shelves of a hidden mini-warehouse.

I laughed at his amazed face. I was sure I'd looked the same way when TL had first shown me the computer lab.

Wirenut stepped through the secret wall. "Optotronics, micromodules, semiconductors, circuit protection, passive components, audio devices, sensors, enclosures, transformers, protoprods…. Do you have any idea"—he picked up a cable—"how much this xial costs?"

TL folded his arms. "Yes, I do. I sign the bills around here."

Wirenut stood there a few seconds, holding the cable,

staring at everything. Then, slowly, he paced down the center of the warehouse and back, scanning the metal racks. "It's everything I've ever wished for. Like Santa dropped the mother lode."

We all laughed.

"You'll have time to look through everything later. Anything else you need, let me or David know, and we'll get it for you. But for now, put down the cable and come on out."

Wirenut put it down, stepped out from the mini-warehouse, and TL showed him how to use the remote control to close the door. We left Wirenut's room and made our way back to the conference room, where we resumed our seats around the table.

TL tilted back in his chair. "I want to express a concern I have."

Wirenut nodded. "Okay."

"You're confident with your abilities. That's good. That's important. But sometimes your confidence comes across as a little too cocky."

Wirenut's brows drew together. Nobody wanted to disappoint TL. "Sir—"

TL held up his hand. "Let me finish."

Wirenut wisely closed his lips.

"I've watched you. I know that when something is requested of you, you become a different person. You become focused. Attentive. Ready."

"You know how to prioritize important things," David added.

Wirenut's face relaxed a bit with their compliments.

"I want you aware of the fact that cockiness and overconfidence can get *any* person into trouble. Fast. Do we understand each other?"

Wirenut nodded. "Yes, sir."

TL was right. Wirenut did come across as cocky sometimes. But it was a funny conceited, not a serious one. It was mostly for show.

"Before a job I always say to myself, 'Game's on. Don't get too confident. Never know what might happen.'" Wirenut shook his head. "Don't know why I just told you that. I guess so you know *I* know that flaw about myself."

"Good. That's good." TL opened the file. "As long as you're aware of your talents and your shortcomings."

"I am."

TL tapped his finger to the open file. "Do any of you know what quid pluolium is?"

We all shook our heads.

"Quid pluolium is a neurotoxin. One drop kills thousands of people."

I blinked. Thousands of people?

"Quid pluolium," TL continued, "is currently under development in a private lab in Rissala. Yesterday, someone broke into that lab and stole half a dozen vials of the toxin."

"Rissala? Where's Rissala?" I asked. Geography had never been my strong point.

"It's a small country located near Greece," David answered me. "It's bordered by the Mediterranean Sea."

TL pulled a piece of paper from his folder and slid it across the table to us. "Whoever stole the toxin left this."

We all leaned in.

"What language is that?" I asked. "What does it say?"

"It's written in Rissalan. Parrot translated it for us. It says that there are three data-encrypted messages hidden throughout the country of Rissala. These messages are some type of computer code. The first message leads to the next, and that one points to the final. The final message reveals where the stolen neurotoxin has been hidden."

Wirenut scoffed. "Sounds like someone's playing a twisted game of cat and mouse."

"Yes, it does," TL agreed.

I raised my hand, my stomach clenching with nerves. "Um, computer code?" I didn't feel good about this.

"You'll be working from home base on this one," TL answered my unspoken question.

I blew out a quiet breath. Home base. Sounded good. Sounded *more* than good.

"Octavias Zorba," TL continued, "is a very wealthy entrepreneur in Rissala. He funded the quid pluolium research and development. He has hired us to find these messages and recover the toxin." TL tapped the paper written in Rissalan. "This says the first encrypted message is hidden in a small ceramic egg in the Museum of Modern Art. Chapling has done some preliminary work and discovered this ceramic egg is protected by the Rayver Security System. As Wirenut knows, he is the only person to have ever broken through the Rayver System."

Wirenut straightened in his chair. "Does this mean I'm going to Rissala?"

TL didn't answer him and instead got really quiet. Seconds passed, and then TL took a breath. "That piece of paper also says that one of the encrypted messages is hidden in the hilt of a seventeenth-century, double-bladed, lion-engraved sword."

Wirenut went very still. I'd never seen him look so paralyzed with fear.

I glanced at David, and he shook his head.

What was going on?

Wirenut shoved back from the table, and I jumped. "Forget it. This is insane. You have to be an *idiot* if you think I'll do this." He jabbed his finger across the table at David and me. "And this is *none* of their business. None of *anyone's* business. Find someone else. I'm not going to Rissala."

3

The following afternoon, I pulled the ranch's van into the high school's lot and parked in the first available spot. I'd had my license for only a week and *loved* being able to drive. It made me feel . . . well, grown up, for lack of a better description. And free.

David, Erin, Adam, myself, and the rest of Team One attended the University of San Belden. Generally, we left there around three and picked up my team from San Belden High. Today, though, David had left classes early because TL had paged him, Erin and Adam didn't have afternoon classes, and the rest of Team One was away on missions. Which left me going to San Belden High alone.

Pocketing the van's keys, I checked my watch. Minutes to spare. I was getting good at this time-management thing. And to think it had once been one of my biggest flaws.

As I climbed out, I caught sight of Wirenut sitting on a bench under a tree. I'd been thinking about him nonstop since yesterday's meeting. He'd been distant last night when I showed him around my lab. I'd seen him this morning at breakfast and wanted to talk to him, but I didn't know what to say. He'd seemed so lost in thought that I figured he needed space. And from his comment at the meeting, he obviously didn't want David and me knowing about his business.

But now, as I approached Wirenut, all my hesitation disappeared. I wanted to be whatever I could for him. A friend, a sounding board, someone he could yell at if need be.

"Hey." I took the wooden bench across from his. "Did your last class get out early?"

"I'm skipping."

"Oh."

I'd never skipped a class in my whole life. I was probably the only person on the planet who actually looked forward to class. Well, except for gym. But then, what nerd *did* look forward to gym?

"You're sitting right outside the school. Aren't you worried about getting caught? TL will be really upset if you get in trouble for skipping. Maybe you should go back in."

"There's only one like it in the whole world," Wirenut mumbled, apparently unfazed by the fact he might get caught cutting. "My dad told me that right before he allowed me to touch the double-bladed, lion-engraved sword. It was one of many unusual weapons he collected."

Unsure of how to respond, I simply sat and listened.

"The cops never found that sword. My testimony put my uncle on death row. I never saw him again. Case closed."

"Testimony?"

Wirenut squeezed his eyes shut, and my heart clinched at the pain evident on his face. "Twelve years ago," he whispered, "I watched my uncle use that same sword to kill my entire family."

My mouth fell open as his words ricocheted through my brain. Twelve years ago he would've been five years old. I'd been nearly the same age when I lost my parents. "Oh, Wirenut." I reached across the bench and gripped his forearm.

He sat frozen, his eyes tightly shut. I could only imagine the horrible, gory scenes flashing through his mind. Images no person, let alone a five-year-old, should ever experience.

Wirenut shook his head, fighting the emotion. I moved beside him and wrapped my arms tightly around him. We stayed that way for a few long minutes, our heads touching as I held him. With all my mental energy, I willed away his horrible memories.

Sometime later he stirred, and I sat back, giving him space.

"I was too young. I couldn't help. How could I have helped? It was impossible." He wasn't talking to me. He was talking to himself, staring at the grass beneath our feet. I didn't know what to say anyway.

Wirenut brought his gaze over to mine. "Don't you think it's weird that my first mission has something to do with my past? Do you think TL knew that when he recruited me?"

Shrugging, I moved back over to my bench. "I doubt it. The neurotoxin was just stolen. But I don't know. It's possible. TL seems to know everything about everybody. I've learned, though, that there's a purpose for the things he does. He wouldn't keep information private unless he had a good reason to do so."

"Maybe there's no stolen neurotoxin. Maybe this is a test to see how I perform under emotional stress. More of my training." Wirenut was talking to himself again, and so I quietly listened.

"No," he said, answering himself. "TL wouldn't stoop to that level. There're other ways to prove my mental stability. Or are there? Challenging someone with their worst fear *is* the ultimate test." He blew out a breath. "A test I'm not ready for."

The bell rang, and students piled out from the high school. Idly, I watched them load into buses, get into cars, and file off down the sidewalks.

Two girls in miniskirts passed by our benches. "Oh, *my* God," one sneered to the other. "Did you see what she was wearing? Puh-lease. Where'd she buy her clothes anyway?"

I sneered right back. They weren't talking about me, but they reminded me of the horrible girls I used to live with in the dorm. They'd made fun of me and it used to intimidate me. Now it just made me angry.

Sensing movement to my right, I glanced up and squinted against the sun.

"Hi!" A brown-haired girl plopped down beside Wirenut.

He flinched from his contemplative state.

"Sixty-four degrees on this beautiful day. Forty percent chance for evening showers. Another gorgeous San Belden, California, day." She stretched her arms over her head.

This must be Nancy. I'd heard my roommates talk a lot about her. She wanted to be a meteorologist and a journalist. They said she started every annoying conversation with a weather report.

Her big yap would make her a better gossip columnist, Wirenut had commented.

I looked over at him. Poor guy. He came out here for a little thinking room, and look who invaded his privacy.

She straightened her shirt. "Did you know one degree Celsius equals Fahrenheit minus thirty-two divided by one point eight?"

Wirenut and I just looked at each other.

"Can you believe we'll graduate high school soon?" She crossed her right leg over her left. "Time just flies, doesn't it? Before you know it we'll be graduating college." Bouncing her crossed leg, she smiled at me. "Are you a new student here?"

"No, I go to the university."

"University? What are you, a freshman?"

"Actually, I'm graduating this year."

She perked up. "You're that whiz kid, aren't you? I've heard all about you. My brother's a junior at the U. He said you're hot."

I felt my face grow warm.

"I bet you didn't have a childhood, did you? How sad." Nancy shook her head, all dramatically concerned. "Kids shouldn't be promoted until they're emotionally ready."

I wasn't sure how to respond, so I glanced at Wirenut. He rolled his eyes.

Nancy inched closer to him, apparently done making small talk with me. With his arms sprawled along the bench's back, they looked more like a couple than tolerant acquaintances.

He dropped his arms and put his book bag between them. If she didn't get the hint from that, I didn't know what to tell her.

"So"—she pushed her sunglasses up her nose—"how do you like it out there at the San Belden Ranch for Boys and Girls?"

A foster home for boys and girls was our cover in the community. If only people knew what *really* went on behind our gates.

"It's all right," Wirenut answered.

"I was thinking about doing an article on all of you for the school paper. Ya know, about how those less fortunate can, if given the proper guidance, turn into fine, upstanding American citizens."

Wirenut rolled his eyes again. "Maybe your ride's waiting for you in the other parking lot."

I almost laughed at the second blatant hint he just dropped.

"Nope. This is the exact spot I'm supposed to be." Nancy sighed. "What is the world coming to? The crime rate these days. You heard about that missing artifact out of New Mexico? What a shame. Happened months and months ago."

Wirenut cleared his throat. "Artifact?"

His slouched posture straightened a little bit. His bored eyes became alert. Small changes that I noticed, but anybody else would say he appeared the same. He was interested in this artifact thing and doing an excellent job of hiding it. TL would be proud.

Nancy finger-fluffed her short hair. "Oh, yeah. But something *really* juicy just came across my desk."

Came across her desk? Who was she, Katie Couric?

Nancy brushed a fallen leaf from her jeans. "It was the Ghost who stole it. You know, the New Mexico thing."

Oh. She was referring to the event that led TL to recruit Wirenut.

"You've heard of him," she whispered, "haven't you? The Ghost?"

Wirenut and I exchanged a quick glance.

Yeah, we've heard of him. He's sitting right beside you.

"No," he responded.

She sucked in a surprised breath. "Well, he's only the most notorious criminal of this century. Some even say he's the most notorious ever."

Wirenut rubbed a hand down his face, hiding his smile. Apparently, his reputation amused him.

"But as I was saying, something really juicy just came across my desk. He just broke into a museum in China and stole another artifact. Apparently this museum in China was supposed to be burglar proof." Nancy glanced around as if the Ghost was going to jump out at her or something. "He's the first to have gotten in."

Wirenut stiffened a little. "How do you know it was the Ghost?"

She wiggled back on the bench, getting comfortable, obviously wallowing in the fact that she was delivering hot-off-the-press news. "His signature."

Wirenut lifted his brows, all nonchalant. "Signature?"

Nancy leaned in. "A yellow ribbon."

Wirenut's jaw tightened.

So, the burglar guy who screwed Wirenut was now impersonating him. Interesting. I wondered if TL knew this. "And how did you get all this information?"

"I told you." She fluffed her hair again. "It came across my desk."

I just looked at her.

"Oh, all right." Nancy waved her hand. "It's in the papers."

"Weeell," drawled Beaker, "isn't this sweet."

Nancy jerked to her side of the bench, straightening her clothes, like she and Wirenut had been messing around or something.

Get a life.

Beaker hitched her chin. "Whaz up?"

Behind her purple-tinted lenses, Nancy narrowed her eyes.

Mystic, Parrot, and Bruiser came out the gym door. Everyone present and accounted for.

I stood and fished the ranch's van keys from my jeans pocket. "Let's go."

"Oh," Nancy extended her hand, "I forgot."

Groan.

She smiled at Wirenut. "Have a good trip."

He frowned. "Trip?"

"Yeah. I'm an assistant in the admin office. I saw your excuse note come over the fax. I figured since you were going to be out of school for a while you were going on a trip." She blinked. "Where are you going?"

Wirenut's face went blank. "Nowhere." He spun and charged off across the parking lot.

We all rushed after him.

"What's going on?" Bruiser asked.

I shook my head. I had the sick feeling TL was sending him to Rissala anyway.

In silence, I drove everyone home. My teammates sat, staring out the windows. I suspected they all knew something major was up. I glanced at Wirenut in the rearview mirror. He hadn't moved from his hard-jawed, arms-crossed, angry position.

I pulled up in front of the ranch's gate. A wooden plaque engraved with SAN BELDEN RANCH FOR BOYS AND GIRLS hung from the entrance.

Keying in my access code, I drove through. A standard privacy fence lined the hundred-acre ranch. Invisible static sensors wound through it, detecting the smallest of movements. No human, animal, or plant could touch it without Chapling knowing. If the electricity went out, generators and solar panels kept the whole ranch active.

To any ordinary visitor the place resembled a nice homey environment for us system kids. Little did anyone know a top-secret, intricate series of sublevels zigzagged the earth below us.

I drove up the driveway and parked in front. Wirenut slung

open the door and jumped out. He stormed across the gravel and into the house.

"Wirenut, stop." I raced to catch up. He ignored me and charged down the hall straight toward TL's office.

"Stop." I cringed, following him. "You're going to get in trouble."

Wirenut slammed through TL's door without knocking. "*What is going on?*"

TL motioned me in, and, silently, I stepped into his office. David stood in the corner, a map in his hands. It'd been only a few hours since I'd seen him, but my stomach still whoop-dee-whooped.

TL leveled unreadable eyes on Wirenut. "Close the door. You three have a seat."

David closed the door, and we each took a metal chair in front of TL's desk.

He pressed a keyboard button and then turned his attention to Wirenut. "I'm assuming you're referring to the Ghost impersonator?" TL shook his head. "Not much I can say about that. Your alter ego is being copycatted."

"I told you," Wirenut forced out through clenched teeth. "I'm not going to Rissala."

TL didn't blink. "I know."

His calm acceptance seemed to zap the rage from Wirenut. He slumped back in his chair. "Then why would Nancy say that?"

"Nancy?" TL asked.

Wirenut shook his head. "A girl at school. She said she saw an excuse note on the fax."

TL nodded. "Yes."

Beside me, Wirenut tensed. "Well? I told you I'm not going."

"I know. David and I are. You have forty-eight hours to train him how to be you. The Ghost."

▓ ▓ ▓

тнат еvеninq I stood in Wirenut's electronics room, idly watching him prepare.

I tried not to be bummed that David would be leaving. I tried to focus on the mission and my part of things. But it just wasn't fair. Other teenagers didn't have to deal with this. They could do what they wanted. They could date and get to know each other without "save the world" pressure. They could go out and have fun. Hang out. Laugh. Just exist. Heck, they could lie around all day and watch TV if they wanted.

"All right," Wirenut interrupted my pouting. "I've turned my room into David's training grounds." He checked his watch. "It's already eight o'clock, and we've got a lot to do. So let's get started." He motioned to the equipment he'd set up in the open area. "TL and I spent the last few hours putting all this together. It's a replica of the Rayver System, complete with lasers and a vault."

David nodded. "Tell me what to do."

Taking a seat in the corner out of their way, I pulled a notepad and pencil from my back pocket. TL told me to take notes. He wanted me aware of all aspects of this mission. I wasn't sure why. After all, I'd be operating from home base, decoding the messages. But I figured TL had his reasons.

"Everything I do is based on degrees. Anybody can jury-rig something, but if done at a different angle, a different degree, you get a completely different result. I'll teach you the Rayver System first, then we'll go over all the possible scenarios you may encounter other than the Rayver System." Wirenut handed David a pair of goggles and tossed a pair to me. "These are fiber-lit. Put 'em on."

All three of us did. Red lasers became visible, zigzagging the area in front of the guys. Cool.

Wirenut nodded toward the lasers. "These will be yellow, not red. But yellow fries your skin. Figured you'd want to train on the nonfrying color."

David chuckled. "Gee, thanks."

Wirenut pulled David over. "Always begin in line with the object you're after. In this case, the vault. Now lean to the left at a seventy-degree angle. Do you see an opening tunnel in the lasers?"

Seventy-degree angle? There's no way I could guess that and get it exactly right.

David leaned. "No."

Wirenut studied David's form. "Your body's twisted. Move your right shoulder back."

David did. "Still don't see it."

Wirenut got in position behind David. "I can see the tunnel

just fine. Your feet are closer together. Slide your left foot to the left seven inches."

"Seven inches?" David glanced over his shoulder at Wirenut. "Do you have a ruler? How do you know this?"

Wirenut shrugged. "I just know."

David slid his foot over. "Okay. I see it."

Wirenut gave David a remote control. "This is the expander. Extend your left arm down the tunnel. Don't touch the lasers."

DingDingDingDingDing.

"That'd be the alarm." Wirenut slapped David on the back. "Let's try again."

▦ ▦ ▦

WIRENUT GAVE DAVID the remote control. "Now extend your left arm down the tunnel, pointing the expander."

I held my breath. They'd been at this more than two hours. Please let him get it right this time.

David inserted his arm into the tunnel surrounded by lasers.

Quiet.

Peace and quiet.

No alarm.

I nearly cried with excitement.

"Keep it steady," Wirenut whispered. "On the expander there is a blue button. When you press it, a metal wire will snake out. The wire cannot touch the lasers. Your destination is that tiny hole below the vault's lock. Do you think you're ready?"

David barely nodded.

"Press the expanding button now."

David pressed the button. The wire snaked out, becoming firm and straight as it left the remote control. One inch. Two. Three. Four. My heart banged with each inch interval. Steady, David, steady.

His hand shook ever so slightly.

DingDingDingDingDing.

Wirenut ran his hand down his goatee. "Let's do it again."

With a huge sigh, David cracked his neck. "Give me a sec." He walked to the other side of the room and stood with his back to us, staring at the wall. I heard him sigh again.

I felt bad for him. He was trying so hard and barely succeeding at anything.

David turned back around. "Okay, let's do this thing."

▓ ▓ ▓

"GOT drinks and sandwiches. Anyone interested?"

David whipped around. "I didn't even hear you leave."

I carried the tray over. The guys had taken only one break since beginning ten hours ago. Both of them looked as exhausted as I felt. And I was just observing and taking notes.

They each grabbed a bologna and cheese sandwich.

"Nothing like bologna for breakfast." David took a huge bite of his. "So, who taught you all this stuff?"

Wirenut popped open a soda. "Nobody. Taught myself. It's my

life. Security, electronics. All I've ever done is study it, tinker with it. It fascinates me." He smiled a little. "And I'm good at it."

"Impressive. Really impressive. We've been at this for hours, and I can't get it. And I'm a real quick study. It's not just about breaking a system. It's about your body's position. The angle at which you do things. It really is incredible, Wirenut. I knew you were skilled, but I didn't understand the scope of it until now."

Wirenut shoved a hunk of sandwich in his mouth, obviously embarrassed, but loving the admiration. His shy avoidance made me grin.

We finished off our sandwiches and downed the sodas.

David and Wirenut got back into position as I gathered up the garbage and headed out the door, dreading what I knew would come next.

DingDingDingDingDing.

⠿ ⠿ ⠿

WIRENUT AND I WATCHED, holding our breaths, as the wire snaked through the tunnel, across the room, and straight into the tiny hole below the vault's lock.

The lasers flicked off, and the three of us just stayed in our spots. Them standing, me sitting. Nobody moving. Unable to wrap our tired brains around the fact that David had done it. He'd actually done it. Finally. After sixteen hours.

Slowly, the guys turned and looked at each other.

"Crud!" Wirenut jerked the stopwatch from his pocket and pressed the button. "Go!"

They raced across the floor, reeling in the expandable wire. Wirenut yanked a tool kit from his back pocket and spread it on the ground in front of the vault.

"Nitrox." He shoved the can at David. "Quick. Got to make up for lost time. Squirt it on the control panel."

David did. The panel popped off and clanged to the floor.

DingDingDingDingDing.

I dropped my head.

Wirenut sighed. "My bad. You have to catch it *before* it hits the floor. Anything over twenty-five decibels sets off the alarm. I'm so tired I forgot that detail."

The door opened and TL stepped into the room. "Chapling downloaded intel. Someone tried to release quid pluolium in an office building."

My stomach tightened. "What? Why?"

"To prove that whoever has the toxin will use it." TL's face hardened. "Thirty-three people almost died. Luckily the toxin was found in time. Give me a status on how David's doing."

We all exchanged defeated gazes. Thirty-three people almost died. If we didn't find the quid pluolium, hundreds, thousands, possibly millions could die.

"I said status. Now."

David took a step forward. "Sir, I haven't been able to penetrate the Rayver System."

And according to Wirenut, the Rayver System was only the beginning. There was so much more to go over. All the different scenarios. There was no way to accomplish it with only hours left of training. Clearly, no one could do this but him.

As if reading my thoughts, Wirenut stepped up beside David. "I'll do it. I'll go to Rissala."

TL nodded, then turned to me. "I asked you to be in here, taking notes, for a reason. You're going with us."

What the . . . ?

maybe i'd heard TL wrong. I pushed up from my spot in the corner. "What do you mean I'm going with you all?"

"The data-encrypted messages, the computer code, is on a timer. We're not sure what kind of timer. Possibly the message disappears? Some sort of chemical reaction to the paper the encryption is on? I've asked Beaker to look into that side of things." TL's cell phone rang. "We need you onsite to immediately decode the data Wirenut obtains."

I *had* heard him right. *Crap.* "But—"

"GiGi," TL checked the caller, but didn't answer, "you'll be fine. You work best under pressure. That's why I waited until now to tell you. You get nervous if you have too much time to think about something."

But you said I would work from home base, I wanted to whine. "What about Chapling?"

"He's working on a couple of other things right now."

Wait a minute. *That's why I waited until now to tell you.* So he'd known days ago that I was going?

Immediately, I recalled all the lies that had originally brought me to the Specialists. Lies that had eventually been justified, sure, but still.

I've learned there's a purpose for the things TL does. He wouldn't keep information private unless he had a good reason. That's what I'd told Wirenut a few days ago. Remembering that rational statement deflated my building irritation.

And TL was right. I *did* work well under pressure. If I had known days ago I would've been obsessing over the trip instead of focusing on the mission.

TL reached out and cupped Wirenut's shoulder. He didn't utter a word as he stared deep into Wirenut's eyes. "I'm proud of you. You put aside your own needs to help others. Only an honorable man would do that. This will be an emotionally difficult mission for you. I realize that. You have my utmost respect for the decision you just made."

Wow. What an awesome compliment.

TL squeezed Wirenut's shoulder and released it. "Get some rest. Our plane for Rissala leaves tomorrow morning."

With that, TL strode from the electronics room. I turned and looked at Wirenut. He stood there, staring at nothing in particular, probably trying to comprehend the mind-numbing words he'd just heard. It's exactly how I felt the first time TL said he was proud of me.

David packed up Wirenut's tool pouch. "It's humbling when he tells you he admires you, isn't it?"

"Man," Wirenut half laughed. "You can say that again."

"Respect goes two ways. He gives it and expects it in return." David flicked off the Rayver System lasers. "You lose it, and it takes forever to get it back."

"Thanks for the warning." Wirenut snatched up his tools. "Catch ya later."

He disappeared through the door, leaving David and me alone.

"Looks like things are reversed now. You're going, and I'm staying." David took my hand. "Don't be nervous."

"Not I'm." I shook my head. "I mean, I'm not." I closed my eyes. I *hated* when nerves made me jumble my words.

I felt him move closer, and I opened my eyes. "What am I going to do? I'll have to get on another plane." And he wouldn't be there like last time.

"You'll be fine. Wirenut will be there. And TL, too."

"They're not you," I whispered.

David's eyes crinkled. "No, they're not. But I'll be there in spirit. Just close your eyes, and I'll be there."

I smiled through a sigh. Months ago I never would've gotten on a plane. I never would've made it over to Ushbania if not for David sitting beside me, holding my hand.

The door opened again, and Erin stepped in. "TL's sending me to town. You two need anything?"

We both shook our heads.

With a nod, she shut the door, leaving us alone again.

David exhaled a heavy breath. "We're always getting interrupted, aren't we?"

I nodded. It did seem like every time we had a moment alone, someone ruined it.

"So, umm, did you two used to date?" It probably wasn't the best time to ask him such a thing.

"We did. For about a month."

"What happened?"

He shook his head. "I've known her a long time. We're friends. We weren't meant to date. There wasn't any chemistry."

Chemistry was the one problem David and I didn't have.

"I was thinking . . ." David ran his thumb over the top of my hand and looked down at my lips.

My stomach did a jig as I recalled the horribly embarrassing kiss I'd given him in Ushbania. "You were thinking?" I croaked.

He closed the small distance between us, putting his face a mere inch from mine.

I shook my head. Hold on. We couldn't kiss yet. I needed to brush my teeth. Our first real kiss had to involve fresh breath. But maybe it doesn't matter—we're finally getting our kiss.

I held my breath and looked into his eyes . . . and then the door opened again and TL stuck his head in. "David, I need you."

My heart paused a beat with disappointment. Yet again I'd have to wait for a kiss.

TL turned to me. "GiGi, the briefing will be back here in thirty minutes."

"Yes, sir."

"When you get back?" David whispered.

I nodded.

He smiled and dropped a quick kiss to my cheek. "Good." Then strode across the room to join TL.

My paused heart kicked to light speed. A kiss. When I got back. Oh boy. How was I supposed to concentrate on the mission with *that* waiting for me?

※ ※ ※

Thirty minutes Later, I walked back into Wirenut's electronics room. TL, David, and Wirenut were already there standing on opposite sides of a tall wooden table.

I stepped up beside Wirenut.

David slid a yellow folder across to me. "In there you'll find your new identity, information on Rissala, and details about the mission."

Opening the folder, I quickly perused the inserted sheets. My name for this assignment would be Dana. Wirenut was Stan, and TL's new name would be Tim. Our cover? Vacationers. Simple enough.

TL opened his file. "To recap. There are three encrypted messages. We know the first one is in the Museum of Modern Art. That message will lead to the next, and that one points to the final. Finding these messages will uncover where the neurotoxin has been hidden."

"We know the first message is protected by the Rayver Security System. We also know the messages are on some sort of timed computer code, which is where GiGi comes in. This code might have to be deciphered right there on the spot. It might not. There could be a delay in satellite transmission, so with everything being on a timer, we don't want to take any chances sending the code back to here." TL clicked his pencil and slid it into the folder's pocket.

Wirenut raised his hand. "Sir, are you saying that GiGi has to go in with me while I break the Rayver System and retrieve the messages?"

"With the timed computer code, we don't know what to expect." TL looked at Wirenut and then me. "So, yes, GiGi will be going in with you."

Wirenut cut me a sideways glance, and I swore he looked a little sick to his stomach.

Come on. I wasn't that bad.

⠿ ⠿ ⠿

ᴇᴀʀʟy ᴛʜᴇ ɴᴇxᴛ ᴍᴏʀɴɪɴɢ. the plane's engines vibrated beneath me, and I shut my eyes.

"You want a sedative?" TL asked from my right.

Shaking my head, I curled my fingers into my thighs.

You can do this. You can.

"It's going to be okay," Wirenut whispered from my left. "Think about computers or something."

Not a bad idea.

I forced my brain to run code.

[%TENLEME sartt:! Q —]

[<& nqouitat - - >tsroh]
[#<#> IUR gsm 118(*)]

The plane picked up speed as it rolled down the runway, and I squeezed my eyes tighter. David's words came back to me. *I'll be there in spirit. Just close your eyes, and I'll be there.*

I conjured his image. Tall, dark, great brown eyes. Wearing his faded jeans and that pale blue T-shirt that hugged his biceps. I saw him laughing, eyes crinkling, flirting with me. His jaw had dark stubble and he smelled . . . heavenly. We'd had a lot of stolen little moments since the Ushbanian mission. Holding hands, talking, a kiss on the cheek. I couldn't wait for the real thing.

The muscles in my body relaxed, and I rested my head back. I opened my eyes and immediately felt both TL and Wirenut looking at me.

"I'm fine," I reassured them.

"Oh, good." Wirenut blew out a dramatic breath. "Didn't want to contend with a puke bag."

I elbowed him.

Wirenut glanced around me to TL. "Thanks for the send-off party."

TL smiled a little. "You're welcome."

I recalled the send-off party they'd given me for my first mission, and how I'd passed out.

TL lowered the window shade, shutting out the sun and clouds. "Long flight to Rissala. Try to sleep."

Hours and hours and *hours* later, our plane began its descent into the capital city. With the time change it was early morning again.

Glancing past TL, I gazed out the window, taking in the scenery. The capital city sprawled across a large cliff, looking out over the sparkling Mediterranean Sea. One-, two-, and three-story stone buildings crammed the cliff, trickling off as the city stretched west from the water. Green hillsides rolled from there with an occasional house or farm.

We took a cab from the airport, zigzagging through a tight maze of the town. The only vehicles I saw were cabs. The few people out and about this early either drove mopeds, rode bicycles, or walked.

Narrow dirt roads led to cobblestone, back into dirt, and then rock. No pavement. The pastel-colored stone buildings sat close to the road with no sidewalks. Our driver honked as we neared a woman, and she plastered herself to the wall.

Roughly fifteen minutes later, we bumped to a stop in front of a two-story tan stone building.

The driver climbed out. "Hotel."

We grabbed our luggage and trucked it through the arched, open doorway. The inside mirrored the stone outside. To the left, a dark-haired woman stood behind a wood counter. She smiled as we approached.

As TL checked us in, I wandered the rustic lobby decorated with bamboo furniture. Paintings with flashes of color in no particular pattern hung on the walls.

"Let's go." TL led the way through the lobby and past an

elevator to the stairwell. We climbed a flight of stairs up to our floor.

"This place has only twelve rooms. Six on bottom, six on top." TL handed me a key. "You're in room ten. We're eleven."

The guys let themselves in their room, and I went into mine. There was nothing unique about it. Tan stone walls and tile floors just like the hallways and lobby. Two double beds with a painting like the ones in the lobby hung above each. A small desk sat between the two beds. A door connected my room to the guys' room.

I peeked in the bathroom. Standard porcelain toilet and sink with a shower stall and no tub.

Crossing the room, I gazed out the small window down to the red-tile roof of a house. A tiny alley separated the two buildings. So tiny I could probably climb out of my window and easily jump down to the roof.

I cranked the knob on the window and let in the fresh cool air. I wished David were here.

A knock on the connecting door brought me out of my thoughts, and I opened it.

TL stepped in. "Upload intel."

Fishing my laptop from my backpack, I quickly connected to the satellite and keyed in the scrambler code. "Nothing new."

TL nodded. "The Museum of Modern Art is a ten-minute walk west of here. There's a café right across from it. Get some breakfast. I have calls to make. I'll meet you two there."

Wirenut stuck his head in. "Did someone say café? Food?"

I laughed. "Let's go."

We left the hotel and walked around the corner to the shadowed side alley. We headed west, away from the sparkling sea. Minutes passed as we strolled, and I trailed my fingers along the stone buildings bordering the street. The texture ranged from gritty to chalky to smooth. The narrowness of the cobblestone path prohibited cars. Only bicycles and the occasional moped zipped past. The city seemed to be waking up, with people opening windows, sweeping their small doorsteps, shaking out blankets.

Pipe music drifted from a couple of the windows. Must be a popular type of music from this area.

Ten minutes later, we neared the café. A green canvas awning billowed out, covering a dozen or so empty wrought-iron tables. Wirenut and I chose one in the center and made ourselves comfortable. Yawning, I closed my eyes, enjoying the early-morning breeze. The scent of fresh baked bread and strong coffee floated through the air.

Wirenut inhaled long and loud, bringing me from my sleepy haze. "Nothing compares to traveling. Seeing cool places. Meeting different people. Trying new foods. Speaking of which . . ." Wirenut signaled the Rissalan waitress.

Before joining the Specialists, adventure was absolute last on my list of things to do. I had to admit, though, being somewhere different *did* excite me. It made me feel like a completely different person.

Smiling, the waitress wound through the outdoor seating

area, her long flowery skirt blowing in the dry, cool air.

She stopped at our table. *"Naz o jimo zua?"* May I help you?

"Oh, yes." I slipped an English/Rissalan dictionary from my back pocket and flipped through it. *"O."* I. Flipflipflip. *"Xuamf."* Would. Flipflipflip. *"Moli."* Like. Flipflipflip. *"E."* A. Flipflipflip. *"Hmett."* Glass. Flipflipflip. *"Ug."* Of. Flipflipflip. *"Odif."* Iced. Flipflipflip. *"Duggii."* Coffee.

I beamed a grin up at the waitress, proud of my bilingual abilities.

"You could've just said *'odif duggii'* and she would've gotten it." Wirenut pointed to the chalkboard menu sitting on the cobblestone walkway. It displayed a breakfast special. *"Qmieti."* He held up two fingers.

With a nod, she made a note on her order pad and headed past us. Wirenut discreetly glanced over his shoulder, looking the waitress up and down as she swerved around a table and entered the restaurant. I smiled to myself and thought again of how much I missed David.

"Mmm-hmm." Wirenut approvingly mumbled of the waitress.

"Hey," I laughed, throwing my napkin at him. "You're here for a reason, remember?"

Grinning, he settled back in his chair. Behind his shades, he surveyed the two-story white stone building that stood across the cobblestone walkway. The Museum of Modern Art.

It wasn't a coincidence TL sent us here. Plenty of time to eat, drink, and get the museum's layout.

A bank stood to the left of the museum and a jewelry store to the right. A sliver of space separated each stone building from the next. Just like both sides of the whole street. Building after building after building. Houses, offices, businesses. It wasn't really beautiful, but more interesting, unique. I'd never been in such a crammed space before.

Sounds of laughter drifted with the wind. I blinked out of mission mode and glanced around. We'd been alone when we first sat down. Now an elderly woman sat to the right and a businessman occupied the table straight ahead.

"Hot chick to the left," Wirenut mumbled.

I glanced over. A sunbeam lit the wrought-iron table where "hot chick" sat alone. She wore a long, gauzy, white skirt, and her straight black hair hung halfway down her back. It blew with the wind, and she held it out of her way while talking with the waitress.

Wirenut was right. "Hot chick" *was* beautiful. With her dark skin and gorgeous smile, she and the waitress could be sisters. Or maybe mother and daughter.

"Hot chick" laughed again. She and the waitress exchanged a few more words in Rissalan, then, carrying her tray, the waitress meandered back over to us. She put our plates and coffees down then pointed to our water glasses. *"Nusi?"* More?

"Pu vjepl vua," Wirenut replied. No, thank you.

We both dove in, forking up big bites of the food Wirenut had ordered us. Fried pork, eggs, and spicy rice. Why didn't they feed us stuff like this at the ranch?

I paused in stuffing my face to take a sip of my iced coffee.

"Please tell me I didn't look like a starving hyena just now."

"Huh?" I glanced over at Wirenut. He was staring at the girl as she stared back at him.

She smiled. *"Jimmu."* Hello.

Wirenut cleared his throat and took a sip. "Don't screw this up," he mumbled to himself. "Play it cool." He sent her a small wave. *"Jimmu."*

"Enisodep?" American?

"Zit." Yes.

"I speak English," she said.

Wirenut smiled, obviously relieved. I mean, how much would that suck? Trying to communicate in Rissalan with somebody you liked. *Hello. Yes. Please. Where's the bathroom?* That conversation would last all of one minute.

"My name is Katarina."

I loved her melodic accent.

"Stan," he introduced, using our fake names. "And this is my *friend,* Dana."

I caught his emphasis on the word *friend,* making sure "hot chick" knew I wasn't his *girl*friend. "Hi."

Wirenut took another bite, chewed. "Ask her a question," he mumbled to me without moving his lips.

Ask her a question? Was he kidding? Conversation was not my strong point. I dug around in my head. *How old are you? Where do you go to school? Come here often?* I nearly laughed at the last one. It sounded like a corny pickup line. And Wirenut was the one picking her up, not me.

"Live around here?" he asked before I had a chance to open my mouth. He shot me a forget-it look.

I shrugged and went back to my food.

She nodded. "On a boat on the canal."

A boat? Neat.

The waitress crossed in front of us. She placed a bowl of fruit on Katarina's table. While they talked, we finished our breakfast.

They shared a laugh, and the waitress looked over her shoulder at us.

"Great. They're talking about us." Wirenut wiped his mouth.

"Hush," I whispered. "They're not talking about us." I thought I was the only one who obsessed about stuff like that.

He propped his feet on the chair beside me. The waitress left Katarina's table, and Wirenut did not hesitate to continue the conversation. "Do you go to school around here?"

"I'm taught at home."

"You mean on the boat?"

She nodded.

"How old are you?"

Katarina cut a chunk of melon in half. "Sixteen. How old are you?"

"Seventeen."

In my peripheral vision a man stopped in front of the museum. Sipping my iced coffee, I studied him. He was the first to show. Must be the manager. I peeked at my watch. 7:05 A.M. Museum opened at 8:00 A.M.

"How long are you here for?" She bit into her melon.

"About a week." Wirenut touched the screw on the right side of his sunglasses, holding his finger there for a count of three. It activated the built-in cameras.

Smooth. I wasn't even sure he'd seen the man. I clicked my watch head twice counterclockwise, engaging the microchip recorder. His glasses contained the same recorder. Mine served as a backup in case something went wrong. The glasses were a nifty little electronic device he had created.

"Are you here with family?" Katarina drank a bit of her hot tea.

"No. Vacation with friends." Wirenut put the glasses on the table and pointed them directly at the museum.

There were two cameras. One filmed the building's exterior, and one, according to Chapling, X-rayed through the stone walls to tape what went on inside.

Katarina pushed back from her table and stood, grabbing her bowl of fruit. She put some bills down and crossed the short distance between us.

Wirenut's jaw twitched as he watched her come toward us. I could only imagine what thoughts spiraled through his head. *Don't go, hot chick. Don't go.*

She extended her hand. "Nice to meet both of you. I wish I had more time to visit."

He shook her hand, looking so bummed I wanted to hug him. "Nice to meet you, too."

Her light brown eyes twinkled. Exotic eyes, kinda catlike. But it was the friendliness of them, the intelligence behind them that caught my attention more than anything, like they invited true, soul-bonding conversation.

She shook my hand. "I'm here every morning for breakfast, if you want to join me sometime. I'd be happy to show you around."

Wirenut's bumminess immediately lifted. "Sounds good."

With another smile, she caught the waitress's eye and held up the bowl. The waitress nodded.

"I'm a regular. They let me take stuff because they know I'll bring it back. Until later." Katarina turned and strolled off down the cobblestone walkway.

Wirenut watched her until she turned the corner and disappeared from sight.

TL passed her coming toward us. He wound around a table, stopping at ours. "Let's go."

Wirenut and I looked at each other. Something wasn't right.

TL put some bills on the table, and we strode off down the cobblestone walkway.

When we got far enough away, TL stopped walking. "Chapling decoded the name of the person who stole the quid pluolium."

Wirenut nodded. "Who is it?"

TL's jaw hardened. "Octavias Zorba. The same man who hired us to find it."

"Oh, my God."

TL turned to Wirenut. "Chapling also uncovered Zorba's real name. It's Antonio Badaduchi. Your uncle."

5

WIRENUT CLENCHED HIS JAW. "That's impossible. My uncle's on death row."

TL glanced down the sunlit cobblestone walkway back to the outdoor café, where more people had gathered. "Come on." He led us down a narrow alley bordered by the back side of a row of stone buildings. From his pants pocket, he pulled out a key chain with a small blue pyramid on it.

Wirenut glanced at it and then did a double take. "That's my white-noise audio-feedback blocker."

I blinked. "Your what?"

TL turned the pyramid's top counterclockwise. "Although no one can detect it, the pyramid emits a static pulse that blocks others from hearing our conversation. Instead of hearing us, they hear white noise."

"You made this?" I leaned in, curious as all get-out.

Wirenut nodded. "Two years ago. I was bored and decided to see if I could do it." He shrugged. "I succeeded."

TL stopped halfway down the alley. He turned and looked at Wirenut.

Seconds ticked by, and, with each one, my heart clanged

harder. When TL stared at you like that, it always preceded life-altering words.

"Your uncle," TL finally spoke, "was never on death row."

It took a pause for Wirenut to comprehend TL's words. "B-but I put him there. I testified against him."

"He was sentenced to death row. But he never made it."

"What do you mean he never made it? He's been on death row for twelve years."

"En route to prison, he was taken by his own men."

"Men? What men? My uncle didn't have men. He managed an antiques store and collected junk."

"That was his cover. He's had his fingers in a lot of illegal stuff."

"That's impossible. I would've known. I was only five, but I would've known. My dad would've known."

TL cupped his shoulder. "I know this is a lot to take in."

Wirenut shrugged away. "Don't talk to me like I'm stupid." He paced a couple of steps. "Let me get this straight. You're telling me that maniac slaughtered my family and has been roaming free every since?"

"Yes."

"Son of a bitch!" Wirenut spun and crashed his fist into the stone building.

I took a step back. I'd never seen him so angry.

"Look at me," TL requested.

Wirenut hit the building again. "Why didn't I know? Somebody should have told me."

TL grabbed his arm. "Look at me," he commanded.

Wirenut opened his eyes.

"We'll get him. You hear me? I promise."

Anger visibly vibrated through Wirenut's body. He stared at TL, shaking, clenching his jaw, his fists, seeming barely to control his fury. "You knew, didn't you? That he never made it to death row."

TL nodded once. "Obviously, though, I had no idea Antonio and Octavias Zorba were one and the same. His identity was hidden deep. I've never even met him. He sent a representative to hire us. And believe me"—TL narrowed his eyes—"I'm *extremely* irritated that I've been duped."

"But you knew," Wirenut gritted, "that he never made it to death row. You should have told me!" Wirenut reared back and rammed his fist into TL's jaw.

I sucked in a breath.

TL barely moved with the impact.

I glanced from TL to Wirenut, and then back to TL. My heart broke with the hurt and sorrow I saw in their eyes.

A split second later, Wirenut bolted down the alley.

I looked at TL and started to go after Wirenut.

"GiGi," TL murmured, "let him go."

▦ ▦ ▦

WIRENUT STAYED GONE the whole day. TL didn't seem to be as worried as I was. As evening approached, I wondered what we would do. According to intel, we had to break into the

Museum of Modern Art that night to retrieve the first encrypted message. Even with all my notes, I knew I couldn't penetrate the Rayver System. We needed Wirenut.

I disconnected the scrambler from the laptop as TL stared at the screen. He'd said barely a word to me since the episode this morning in the alley. Normally, I didn't mind silence, but this was driving me mildly insane.

"What are we going to do if Wirenut doesn't show up?"

TL shook his head. "He'll come back."

"What about Octavias Zorba?"

"He doesn't know that we know he stole the toxin. He doesn't know that we know he's Wirenut's uncle." TL rubbed his hand across his jaw. "We're going to do the only thing we can do. Decipher these encrypted messages, find the neurotoxin, and bring Octavias down."

"But what if it's all a trap?"

TL sighed. "It probably is. That's why we've got the best people on our side. We'll stay one step ahead of Octavias."

Someone rapped on the hotel door six quick times (our secret knock). Wirenut. Thank God.

Sliding my glasses to the top of my head, I looked away from the laptop as he let himself in. Poor guy. He looked so worn-out. Being on an emotional roller coaster does that to a person. I just wanted to hug him.

TL didn't move from his spot next to me, just kept studying the screen. "We move out in one hour."

"What if I hadn't come back?"

TL still didn't look at him. "I knew you would."

All of us, actually, had been on an emotional roller coaster since joining the Specialists: being recruited by TL, settling into our new lives, forming trusting friendships and family-type bonds. But Wirenut . . . this first mission connected to the single most horrible event of his life. How huge. Was there anything else TL was hiding from him?

Wirenut trudged across the room and settled right behind us on the edge of the bed. He studied his lap.

TL finally turned.

Wirenut brought his eyes up. "I'm sorry."

"Apology accepted." TL tapped his jaw where Wirenut had hit him. "That was your free one. Punch me again, and I *will* punch back."

"Yes, sir."

"It takes a real man to apologize."

Tears filled Wirenut's eyes, and he lowered his head.

I sniffed back my own tears, glad they were making up.

TL smiled a little. "It's okay to cry."

Wirenut laughed humorlessly. "Jeez, man, don't you stop?" He scrubbed his eyes. "I'm fine."

"Is there anything you want to ask me?"

Nodding, Wirenut lifted his head. "Why didn't you tell me my uncle never made it to death row?"

"Part of my job involves secrets and knowing when to tell those secrets. Oftentimes it hurts people I care for, and I am sorry for that. Believe me when I say I tell you things when it's the right time for you to know. I wanted you to be mature enough to handle it. After the conversation we just had, I have no doubt you are."

Wirenut pressed his fingers to his eyes. "I'm acting like such a girl."

"Hey," I said jokingly, defending all girls.

Chuckling, TL sat down beside Wirenut. He looped his arms around both of our necks and pulled us in for a quick hug. "The good news is that we know your uncle's identity now. That man has been at large for twelve years. He's finally going to pay for what he did to your family."

⸭ ⸭ ⸭

One hour later, I lay belly down on the museum's brown-tile roof. Getting up here had been much easier than I thought. Stairs led up from the back.

I watched as Wirenut chiseled a notch six inches northeast of the roof's one and only window.

He looked over at me and grinned.

Bingo.

Double-coated EDF wire.

With a lighter, he melted two drops of copper onto the wire. The combination of the two short-circuited, and the window popped open.

He shook his head. "Accu Security. Come on, people, update your technology. This hit the market three years ago."

He packed up his tools while I secured the small foldable

satellite dish to the roof. We pulled our hoods down over our faces. He tossed a rope through the roof window, and we dropped eight feet to the floor of a cleaning closet.

"Okay, game's on. Don't get too confident. Never know what might happen."

Pressing the talk button on my vest, I activated my tooth mike. "We're in." I checked my watch. "Twenty-three oh-three hours."

"Copy that," TL answered into my ear transceiver, from his lookout spot outside the museum.

Quickly, I recalled the blueprints I'd memorized. The upstairs of the 3,000-square-foot building served as offices and storage, and downstairs was the museum. We needed to go down one flight and hang a right.

On silent, slippered feet, we shuffled out of the closet and down the marble hall to the stairs. In the dimly lit hallway, I studied the descending treads. Probably rigged with weight sensors. Wirenut had said buildings that still used the Accu system on the roof window would have weight sensors on the stairs. They came in the same security package.

Which meant the wooden banister was our only way down.

Wirenut hopped up, struck a surfer pose, and slid all the way down. He sailed off the end and quietly landed on his feet.

He turned and bowed, all full of himself, then motioned me on. If he thought I was surfing the banister, he was sadly mistaken. *Need I remind him I'm a total klutz?*

I climbed on, straddling the banister very grannylike, and slid down to where he stood.

We crossed the marble foyer and came to a stop in the pottery room's doorway. The ceramic egg that held the first encrypted message sat on a stand in the room's center. A glass box encased it.

That's worth millions? You've got to be kidding me.

Taking a moment, I ran my gaze around the room, passing over wall-mounted, ceramic figurines. It didn't seem like there was anything unusual, except the egg wasn't in a vault, which was supposed to be part of the Rayver Security System.

But I wasn't the expert here. Wirenut was.

This was as far as I went. It's up to him now. I reached inside my vest for the mini-laptop.

A shadow flickered, and my gaze jumped to the other side of the room. I froze.

Another person. Dressed just like us.

I looked at Wirenut and he tensed up. "It's him," he whispered.

Oh, my God, this must be the other burglar. The one who got Wirenut busted. The same one who impersonated him in China.

"I knew you'd be here." Some sort of voice box warbled his actual speech.

He knew we'd be here?

The burglar took the fiber-lit goggles from the top of his hood-covered head and fit them over his eyes.

We did the same with ours. Yellow lasers spanned the distance between us and where he stood on the other side of the room. The ceramic egg sat smack dab between us. Through the lasers' crisp, zigzagging pattern, I watched the burglar pull a remote control expander from a pocket on the calf of his pants.

Not only did he dress the same as Wirenut, but he kept his tools in the same locations. Complete, sneaky copycat.

"Can he disengage the Rayver System from that side, too?" I whispered.

Wirenut nodded. "There're two locks. One on each side. Some Rayver System setups have that option."

The burglar pointed to the egg, then to his chest. *Mine.*

My jaw dropped. The nerve.

Wirenut got his remote-control expander, and they both moved at once.

My pulse jumped.

Leaning to the left at a seventy-degree angle, Wirenut spied his opening tunnel. He pointed the control down the tunnel and pressed the expanding button. The skinny, metal wire snaked out.

Steady, Wirenut, steady.

I switched my gaze across the room to the burglar. Through the field of lasers, I watched him perform the mirror image of Wirenut's actions. I looked at his wire snaking out and then at Wirenut's, which appeared to be a fraction ahead of the burglar's.

Wirenut's wire connected with the hole below the stand's lock, and the lasers flicked off.

The yellow sizzlers on the burglar's half of the room stayed on. *Yep, we're definitely ahead of him.*

His lasers flicked off.

Crap, not as far ahead as I'd hoped.

Wirenut set his watch, and so did I. One minute and seventeen seconds until everything turned back on. Reeling in the expandable wire, he sprinted to the middle of the room. He yanked the tool kit from his vest and spread it out on the stone floor.

A mere foot of space separated him from the burglar. Wirenut crouched on one side of the stand and the burglar on the other. Wirenut could reach out and strangle him they were so close.

Taking the nitrox first, Wirenut squirted the control panel below the lock. It popped off, and he caught it. Multicolored wires crisscrossed one another. He grabbed the diversion and ripped them out.

The burglar's clump landed right beside Wirenut's.

Jeez, the other guy's quick.

Wirenut took his extra-long, needle-nose wire cutters and, leaning to the left, found his tunnel through the red lasers. He inserted the cutters and snipped the white wire at the very back.

ClickClick. Their locks opened simultaneously.

Come on, Wirenut. Come on.

Grrrgrrr.

Wait. There shouldn't be a *grrrgrrr.* That wasn't the right sound.

The burglar reached for the protective glass. Wirenut stretched around the stand and quickly seized the burglar's wrist.

"It's a trap," Wirenut whispered.

He held his hand up to the burglar. *Don't move.*

I barely breathed as I watched Wirenut dig in his vest. This was what he meant when he said there were all kinds of scenarios that could happen. As good as David was, there was no way he could've learned everything in such a short time.

Wirenut slipped mini–jumper cables from his vest. He clipped one end to the control panel, leaned around the stand, and clipped the other end to the burglar's control panel. I knew from our hours of training that the two connections would cancel each other out and disconnect the alarm.

Lifting the glass, Wirenut snatched the ceramic egg. He unclipped the cables and swept up his tools. He dashed across the open floor back to me, with the burglar right on his heels. They both dove, and the yellow lasers flicked on behind them.

The burglar tackled Wirenut, and I tackled the burglar. The three of us rolled across the marble foyer. The ceramic egg flew through the air. The burglar kidney-punched Wirenut and then head-butted me, stunning me for a quick second. Just enough time for him to scramble out between us and across the floor.

"You broke it," he hissed, holding up half the egg.

Wirenut pushed to his knees, grasping the other half. "Give me what's inside, and you can have this half."

It took the burglar a second to understand. He looked into his half, reached in, and pulled out a small piece of paper. He held it up. "What is it?"

"None of your business," Wirenut snapped.

People's lives depended on that message. We had to get it.

"Listen, you would've set off the alarm back there if it wasn't for my partner. Now give us that paper."

The burglar studied the scrap as if he thought he had some negotiating power here.

Give us that paper or you're going down.

Putting his half of the egg in his vest, he held out the paper. "Count of three, you give me your half, I'll give you this paper."

Wirenut nodded. "One, two, three."

They quickly exchanged, and the burglar jumped on the banister and climbed it to the top floor. Obviously, he knew about the stairs' weight sensors.

Wirenut handed me the paper. "Hurry."

I pulled out my mini-laptop and quickly punched in the encrypted computer code. A series of numbers. As I keyed, the numbers began to slowly fade. "Oh, no." I typed faster, staring at the paper, memorizing the strands near the end that were almost gone.

"What is it?" Wirenut leaned over me. "Oh, crud. Already?"

I shook my head, keying faster, finishing up from memory.

Wirenut pressed the talk button on his vest. "Message secured. Taking alternate route out." He released the talk button.

"We're not going out the roof window. That dude screwed me the last time I followed him. Not again. Let's go."

I followed Wirenut past the stairwell, through a room with modern steel sculptures, and out into a back hall. He clipped a white wire in the corner of a window frame and slid the glass up.

I climbed through first, and Wirenut followed. TL met us in the dark alley outside. Quickly, we filled him in on the burglar and the disappearing message. Then we slipped our street clothes on over our black outfits and, in the midnight moonlight, made our way back through town.

I ran the encrypted numbers through my head, analyzing the strands, the sequences. I itched to get to the hotel, contact Chapling, and crank up my laptop.

Ten minutes later, we walked into TL's and Wirenut's hotel room. TL activated the blue pyramid audio-blocker so no one could hear what we were doing.

Slipping on my glasses, I powered up my laptop and got down to work. I sent Chapling the encrypted message.

GOT IT, he typed back. THOUGHTS?

THE DE NUOWSI'T THEOREM, I answered. It had hit me during our walk through town. The De Nuowsi't theorem was a mathematical code that translated to letters. There were lots of theorems like this used for computer language, but the De Nuowsi't one was created by a man who lived right here in the Mediterranean.

SMARTGIRLSMARTGIRL, Chapling typed.

A few seconds passed while I waited for his comments.

TRIWALL, he typed.

Huh. I didn't expect the theorem to be protected. GIVE ME A SEC, I responded, running code through my brain.

More seconds passed, or maybe minutes.

And then it hit me. TRY <Ide>4</Ide><sni>6/sni>, <...=yoj-liki+[#@jum%^]>

OH YEAH. YOU'RE GOOD. GOODGOOD.

I smiled.

"David," TL spoke into his cell phone, and my ears perked up. "Get me anything you can on this Ghost impersonator and why he would be after the same thing we are. And how he knew we were going to be there. See if Beaker has anything on this disappearing message. What kinds of chemicals would cause it and what can we do to stop it? Also, contact Octavias Zorba and arrange a meeting. He has no idea we know who he really is." TL clicked off. "Now we wait for our guys back home to come through."

At this point there really wasn't much I could do but wait for Chapling to run the encrypted message through the De Nuowsi't theorem. So I logged onto e-mail and smiled when I saw David's name. I clicked on the message:

"Hi. Just wanted to make sure you made it safe and sound. How'd your flight go? Miss you. D."

I glanced over my shoulder to make sure TL and Wirenut weren't watching and typed back:

"Hi! Flight went good. I did exactly what you said. I thought of you. It worked. I miss you, too. A lot. GiGi."

I read what I'd typed, deleted the "A lot," and hit send. "A lot" seemed too much.

HERE YOU GO. Chapling IMed me and sent the decoded encryption.

"I got it," I told TL. "Chapling's sending it right now."

TL and Wirenut leaned in to look at the laptop.

RISSALA MUSEUM OF HISTORY. KING'S CROWN.

USE ELEMENTS TO RETRIEVE DATA.

"Elements?" I asked.

TL rubbed his chin, thinking. "Chemicals. It's telling us we'll have to chemically treat the crown to retrieve the encrypted data." He touched my shoulder. "Give me everything you can on that crown. I'll get Beaker busy on chemical analysis."

⠿ ⠿ ⠿

TL had an early-morning meeting with a local agent. He sent Wirenut and me to check out the Rissala Museum of History.

So here we sat on the hilltop above the capital city, watching the early sun peek out over the Mediterranean Sea. It was the most beautiful clear blue water I'd ever seen. From our high vantage point I scanned the canals, idly watching the boats sway in the gentle breeze. Below us the city crammed the cliffs. Our hotel was smooshed in there somewhere. It'd been quite a climb getting up here.

Beside me, Wirenut zipped up his windbreaker halfway. "A little chillier this morning than yesterday. In an hour it'll be just as warm. No rain expected."

"You sound like Nancy."

He laughed at that and pointed in the distance to the boats that lined the canals. "You suppose that's where Katarina lives?"

"What are you doing thinking about her?"

Playfully, he shoved my head. "Nothing. Shut up. I shouldn't have said anything."

I shoved him back. "Oooh, Wirenut's got a crush on a girl."

He rolled his eyes and made a face.

Laughing, I shaded my face from the brightening sun and squinted down the hill at a one-room, pastel green stone building. The Museum of History.

I took a swig of the now-cold coffee I'd gotten from the hotel. Beside me Wirenut popped a chocolate-covered espresso bean in his mouth. "I've crossed the tired zone into punchy exhaustion."

I eyed his espresso beans. "Where'd you get those?"

"I brought them with me." He held out his hand. "Want some?"

"Sure." I grabbed a handful.

Wirenut popped another espresso bean. "Maybe I should just hook up to a caffeine IV."

I smiled a little. "Chapling's rubbing off on you."

Wirenut slipped the paper cup from my hand and sipped. "Uck. Cold."

I checked my watch. 7:30 A.M. "You got everything you need?" We'd been here on the hilltop above the city since predawn getting the layout for tonight's break-in into the Museum of History.

Wirenut nodded. "Let's hit that café again. I'm starving."

We pushed up from the ground and made our way down the winding dirt road. Tiny white stone cottages dotted the hillside. The buildings' doors signified the only colors. Bright blues and reds.

Other than the little houses, the museum, and a cemetery, nothing existed on the hillside.

A movement off to the left drew my attention. I looked and saw . . . *Katarina?* Wirenut must have seen her, too, because he stopped walking.

"Let's go say hi." He crossed the dirt road.

"She's praying," I whispered, but followed him anyway.

We stepped through the cemetery's arched gate and stopped about ten feet away at a mausoleum.

In the sparse brown grass, Katarina knelt next to a grave with her head bowed. She glanced over her shoulder at us.

Her eyes smiled, and she softly waved at us. We stayed at the mausoleum until Katarina was finished.

"Hi," she whispered as she approached. "I was just visiting my mother. She died when I was a little girl."

"M-my mother died, too," Wirenut murmured.

She looked up at him, surprise obvious in her eyes. I decided to stay silent. It seemed as if they were having a private conversation. I felt like I should leave and give them time alone, but I couldn't make myself walk away.

I missed David.

"What'd you do?" Katarina changed the subject, pointing to the red, scabby marks on Wirenut's right hand.

"I got mad and hit the side of a building."

"Hmmm…well, remind me never to make you mad."

"I've never gotten that way before. Really. I hope it doesn't scare you."

She shook her head, smiling. "I'm not scared." She slid her straw purse onto her shoulder and looked at me. "Café?"

I returned her contagious smile. No wonder Wirenut was so drawn to her. "That's where we were heading."

We exited the cemetery and strolled past the Museum of History.

Katarina rubbed her chin. "I like this on you, Stan. This . . . this . . . Oh, how do you say it in English?"

"Goatee."

"Goatee, right. It's sexy."

He glanced away, and I pressed my lips together to hold my smile. Sometimes I wished I could be that direct.

She bumped his shoulder with hers. "Did I embarrass you?"

He laughed. "Yeah, actually, you did."

Katarina laughed, too. "I'm sorry." She repositioned her purse on her shoulder. "I'm going to the marketplace later, if you want to join me. It's along the cliffs. I'll be there around lunchtime."

Wirenut nodded. "Sounds good."

In content companionship we continued strolling down the hillside road to the outskirts of the city. We rounded the corner onto a street.

"Qeqis!" Paper! shouted a kid, waving today's edition.

"Just a second." Katarina dug a coin from her purse and gave it to the boy. "My father wanted me to buy one." She opened the folded newspaper, perused it.

I peered over her shoulder at the Rissalan headlines. "What does it say?"

"Yellow ribbon says the Ghost strikes again."

Wirenut and I exchanged a quick look. He hadn't left a yellow ribbon last night. The burglar must have.

Crap.

6

THIRTY MINUTES LATER, after a quick breakfast at the café, we strode into Wirenut's and TL's hotel room.

Wirenut tossed the newspaper onto the bed. "Have you seen the headlines?"

TL didn't turn from staring out the small window. "Yes."

"We didn't leave a yellow ribbon."

"Of course you didn't." TL lifted a hotel mug to his mouth and took a sip. From the square of paper dangling off the edge, I assumed it contained hot tea. "I've decided we're going to catch the burglar."

Wirenut perked up. "Really?"

TL moved from the window. "My gut tells me he's going to be at the Museum of History tonight. After the king's crown, just like us. He's involved with Octavias Zorba. Has to be. Catching the burglar, the Ghost impersonator, will lead us to Zorba."

I sat down on the bed. "Did David get the meeting scheduled with Zorba?"

TL dunked his tea bag a couple of times. "No. Zorba is conveniently out of town on business. He won't be back for weeks. I've got David working on where exactly this business is."

"What about the burglar?" I crossed my legs. "Anything on him?"

"Just that he's been impersonating the Ghost all over the place. He did a job in Australia a few weeks ago. Left a yellow ribbon and all." TL shook his head. "Whoever he is, his identity has been hidden well."

"Want me to get cranking on it?" I asked.

"No. Chapling's got it under control. What about the crown?"

I nodded. "I've got all the information."

"Good. We'll put it all together later in a conference call."

Wirenut folded his arms across his chest. "How are we going to catch the guy?"

"We're going to get the king's crown with the encrypted message. Then we'll sit back and wait for the burglar to show."

Wirenut plopped down beside me on the bed. "What do we do for the day? Sit around here?"

TL put his mug down on the windowsill. "I've got another meeting with a local agent. You two enjoy a little scenery. There's nothing to do until tonight."

"There's a marketplace along the cliffs," Wirenut suggested. "Mind if we go there?"

I held in a knowing smile. The marketplace where Katarina would be.

"That's fine." TL tucked his wallet down his back pocket. "Make sure you have your cell phones with you at all times."

▦ ▦ ▦

WIRENUT AND I LEFT the hotel and walked east through town toward the sea. About ten minutes later, we reached an outdoor market that stretched for almost a mile along one of the cliffs. According to the lady at the hotel, everybody made a stop at the marketplace for daily goods.

We wove through the crowded walkways, wandering the cobblestone paths, taking in all the interesting stalls. Clothes, handmade toys, fresh fruits and vegetables, purses, hats. I bought some figs, wishing I could find a stand that sold lollipops.

Soft music trickled somewhere in the distance. "Do you hear that?"

Wirenut strained to listen over the crowd. "Yeah."

"Oooh," a tourist behind me cooed in English. "That's Gio. I saw him perform yesterday. He's really good." She pushed between me and Wirenut, pulling her friend with her. "Excuse us."

"Gio." Wirenut grumbled. "Probably some sexy musician. Why do girls always think musicians are hot? I need to learn an instrument. Something manly. Saxophone, drums, guitar. Whadaya think?"

True. Musicians *were* hot. "Saxophone."

Through the crowd we followed the two girls as the music got louder and louder. In the center of the street a small group had gathered. On a stool in the middle sat the oldest man I'd ever seen. He held a small weird-looking guitar.

I glanced at Wirenut. "Sexy."

He smiled sarcastically.

A dark-haired girl knelt beside the old man. I studied her a second, realizing, "That's Katarina."

Wirenut perked up.

The old man handed her tiny silver cymbals that she slipped onto her middle fingers and thumbs.

Neat. She was about to perform.

She kissed him on both cheeks, and his face brightened into a wrinkly grin.

Gio began strumming the odd guitar, using all his fingers to go up and down the strings. A mellow, hypnotic beat emerged. I watched him for a second or two, then switched my full attention to Katarina.

She stood with her eyes closed, head back, one hand extended above her head and the other down by her side. Her sandaled feet were tight against each other, and her knees bent slightly. She was beautiful.

Gio began singing in Rissalan. A sad song in a tenor's voice.

Katarina's hips slowly rotated. Gently, she tapped the cymbals together. *Taptap taptap*. With her eyes still closed, she brought the hand extended in the air down in front of her face, trailed it between her breasts, over her stomach, and across her hips.

Her eyes snapped open at the exact second Gio upped the rhythm.

She whirled away, tapping the cymbals to Gio's beat. Her long black hair and loose burgundy skirt flowed with every movement.

Katarina circled Gio and then came straight toward us.

Leveling her eyes on Wirenut, she crooked her finger. He stepped from the small group.

She trailed her hand down his bare arm and clasped the tips of his fingers, pulling him into the center of the group.

She circled around him, *taptap taptap*, crossed her arms, *taptap taptap*, moved them at different angles, *taptap taptap*. He followed her movement with his eyes.

Her skirt swept his legs. Her hair brushed his arms. She closed her eyes, *taptap taptap*, then opened them and gazed straight into his.

Strangely enough, he didn't look nervous. More hypnotized than anything else. Totally blocked to anything but her. I couldn't fathom performing that dance, alone or in a crowd.

The music came to an end, and I applauded along with the small gathering. We all tossed coins into Gio's guitar case.

I walked up to Wirenut, who hadn't moved since the music stopped.

"Hi." I greeted Katarina.

She kissed my right cheek and then my left. She did the same to Wirenut, and he grinned. He had it bad for this girl.

Katarina slipped the tiny cymbals from her fingers. "That was the Sotrys. It's the oldest Rissalan dance. I perform it almost every week with Gio. What'd you think?"

"It's gorgeous," I answered.

"Wow." Wirenut shook his head. "That was . . . wow."

Katarina and I laughed.

"Do the girls dance like that in America?"

Wirenut blew out a breath. "None that I know."

"Come. I want you to meet Gio." She handed the old man the cymbals. *"Vjiti esi na gsoipft, Stan epf Dana.* These are my friends, Stan and Dana," she translated.

He extended his weathered hand, and we shook it.

"Gio mowit up vji cuev piyv vu uast. Gio lives on the boat next to ours."

The old man nodded. *"Jux na gevjis ot?"*

"He asked how my father is." Sadness replaced her carefree mood. *"Vufez't e huuf fez.* Today's a good day."

Gio began strumming his guitar as another small group formed around him. *"Vimm jon vjeplt gus vji muctvis."*

"Tell him thanks for the lobster," she interpreted, then kissed the old man good-bye. *"O xomm.* I will."

"Is your father okay?" I asked Katarina after we left the small group, although I knew something wasn't right.

She lowered her gaze to the cobblestone beneath our feet. "He has a brain tumor. Doctors have given him six months."

Whoa. "Are you okay?" Stupid question. Of course she wasn't okay. Her mother's dead, and her father's about to die.

Katarina gave us a somber smile. "Actually, I am okay. I've known for a while and have had time to adjust."

Wirenut put a comforting arm around her. "Who are you gonna live with?"

She wrapped her arm around his waist. "My uncle and aunt."

We crossed through a tent filled with hats and clothes.

"You mentioned lobster. Is that what your dad does?" It made sense. People who lived on boats probably fished for a living.

"No. My father's a businessman. Investments, real estate, and more, but I don't keep up with it."

Businessman and boat living didn't go together in my mind.

Katarina smiled. "Anyway, what happened this morning? You took off so quick."

"We," I fibbed, "remembered something we were supposed to do."

"Oh." She waved around the marketplace. "Mind if I join you?"

Wirenut stepped to the side. "Lead the way."

We followed her off the sunlit sidewalk and ducked into a shaded tent filled with bright silks. She raised her hand in greeting. *"Jimmu."*

From the other side of a table, a small girl grinned. *"Jimmu, Katarina. Jux esi zua?"*

Katarina nodded. *"Gopi. Vjepl zua. Fu zua piif epzvjoph?"*

The girl shook her head. *"Pu."*

From my back pocket, I pulled out my English/Rissalan dictionary and began flipping through it.

Katarina tapped the dictionary. "She asked me how I was and I told her fine. Then I asked her if she needed anything, and she said no."

I laughed. "Thanks."

The girl nodded to another customer, and they began discussing the fabrics. Or at least I assumed they were discussing fabrics.

Katarina trailed a finger down a bundle of white silk. "Her name's Rashon. She runs her family's business."

I glanced over at the shiny-faced, happy girl. "She runs the business? She's just a kid."

"Twelve."

Wow. That's a lot of responsibility for a twelve-year-old. Then again, at twelve I was being watched by the government for recruitment. Who would've figured?

Katarina waved good-bye to the little girl and led the way from the shaded tent back onto the sunlit cobblestone walkway. "I just wanted to check in on her. Oh, look." She stopped at a tattoo booth.

Behind the small table sat a . . . well, I suppose "a warrior" described him best. Large, muscular, no shirt, long dreadlocks, Polynesian. Ancient tribal tattoos decorated his face. He worked on a woman's back, designing a snake.

"I *love* tattoos. I'd never get one. I'm too much of a wimp for the needles. But I *love* them." Katarina whipped around as if suddenly struck by a thought. "Does either of you have one?"

I shook my head. "I'm a wimp, too."

Wirenut lifted his T-shirt sleeve and showed her the thorn tattoo circling his upper bicep. I remembered the first time I met him, I thought it was the coolest thing.

She traced her finger all the way around it and looked up at Wirenut.

Okay, time for me to make my exit. These two needed to be alone. "I'm, um, going to check out the jewelry."

Without taking her eyes off Wirenut, Katarina nodded. "The jewelry lady hand makes each item."

I crossed the cobblestone path. An old, sun-charred lady sat on the ground twining gold wire. Necklaces and earrings decorated the blanket surrounding her, each one unique in its own way. Kneeling, I fingered a row of silver earrings.

I glanced over my shoulder back to the tattoo booth. Wirenut and Katarina had gone. With a smile to the jewelry lady, I got to my feet and headed from the marketplace.

Outside the market I spotted Wirenut and Katarina sitting beneath an olive tree on a cliff. The ocean stretched in front of them, sparkling in the sun. A constant dry, warm breeze blew the water's salty scent past. Neither of them spoke as they watched dolphins lazily peak the blue horizon. Muted sounds from the marketplace flowed past.

Comfortable. Content. Cozy. Words that streamed through my mind as I watched the two of them. They couldn't have asked for a better romantic afternoon.

God, I missed David.

They glanced at each other, lips curved slightly. Lifting his hand, he tucked her dark hair behind her ear and asked her something. With a smile, she nodded.

Bbbzzzbbbzzzbbbzzz.

They jumped apart, and I snapped from my trance.

Our phones. With a quick glance at the *** readout, TL's code, I strode down the hill to where Wirenut and Katarina sat.

Clenching his jaw, Wirenut snapped his cell off his pants and checked the display. He turned to Katarina. "I'm really sorry."

"It's all right." She pushed up off the ground. "I have to go anyway."

He helped her up. "Café? Tomorrow morning?"

She smiled. "Sure."

I didn't want to remind him that we might not even be here tomorrow morning. Somehow, though, I knew that wouldn't matter to him.

As she strolled away from us along the cliff, Wirenut put his hand over his heart. "That smile shot straight through me."

"Bummer she's here and you live in California."

Ignoring my comment, Wirenut and I took off in the opposite direction back into the outdoor market toward our hotel. "She's so perfect. I've never clicked with anyone like I have with her. And I've had only three conversations with her." He half laughed. "Go figure. I asked her if I could kiss her. I've never asked any girl that question before."

I smiled. It reminded me of David. He told me he never kissed a girl unless he knew she wanted to be kissed.

Our phones buzzed again with urgency, and we took off running.

WIRENUT AND I RUSHED into the hotel room.

TL sat at the desk between the two beds. "Conference call. Now." He activated the pyramid-shaped audio-feedback blocker in case someone passed by in the hall.

Wirenut and I situated ourselves on either side of him on the beds. TL ran his finger across the laptop's touch pad, and the screen flickered on.

Chapling's, Beaker's, and David's faces appeared, transmitted via satellite.

David looked right at me, and his eyes crinkled. I smiled as my stomach jingle-jangled.

Chapling waved. Next to him, Beaker remained blank-faced. She'd dyed her green hair black, and I wondered, as I had many times before, what her natural color was.

A five-pointed crown popped up on the bottom left corner of the screen.

"Here's the crown you're after tonight," Chapling began. "This belonged to the first king of Rissala. It's currently located in the Museum of History and holds the next encrypted message. GiGi, tell us what you found out."

I slipped on my glasses. "I input the crown's dimensions into the SNI system and coded the chemical makeup I found on file. I interpreted the history and prohibited rendering of visual framework. Attributes of the ID class were discouraged, but I forced a break by controlling the elements. Traditionally, intrinsic scripts render subsequences. But after only a few moments, I addressed the stylistic treatment of pontdu. So that's no longer an issue. However, with quote blocks marching orcs, we secured a designated source document. Abbreviated text shows—"

"Uh," David stuck his finger in the air, "you lost me way back at the crown's dimensions." He patted his T-shirt pocket. "And I forgot my secret decoder ring. Can you make it simple for me? For us?"

This happened all the time with me. "Oh, right. Sorry."

Chomping her gum, Beaker snorted.

Chapling perked up. "I understood you."

I gave him a thank-you-but-of-course-you-understood-me-you're-a-nerd-too smile.

He bounced his bushy red brows, and I silently laughed. I adored Chapling.

TL shifted. "You're doing fine, GiGi. Finish up."

I took a second to ungeek all the mumble jumble in my brain. "After digging through various online archives, I discovered crowns have been used for centuries to hide objects. The encrypted message should be located in one of the jewels decorating the crown's five points. We don't have time to remove the jewels and break them all open. Beaker, this is where you come in."

With a nod, Beaker took the gum out of her mouth. "Each crown point has a ruby and an emerald. One drop of barium gentrea will expose any imperfection in a ruby. Two drops of carmine nitrate will take care of the emeralds. I suggest you try the rubies first. My research revealed that more people embed messages in those than in emeralds because rubies are easier to manipulate. Once they're transparent you can see which one hides the message. Voilà. Nothing fancy about it." She tossed her gum back in her mouth.

"What about the encrypted message?" I asked. "The fading. Anything on that yet?"

"Oxygen activates it." She shook her head. "That's all I know. I don't know how to stop it. Sorry. You'll just have to work quickly."

"That's all right," TL said. "GiGi did it last time. She can do it again."

Nothing like pressure.

"Where do we get these chemicals for the gems?" asked Wirenut.

"We have a local contact. I'll take care of it." TL reached for the laptop. "Still nothing on the burglar's identity?"

Chapling shook his head.

"Okay. Signing off." TL pressed the escape key, and the screen went black.

I didn't even have a chance to look at David one last time.

⊞ ⊞ ⊞

THAT EVENING, WIRENUT AND I knelt behind a gravestone, scoping out the back side of the Museum of History. Three entrance possibilities: front door, side window, rear door. No other entry points existed on the one-room stone structure.

To the untrained, the building had the lure of an easy job. The old *looks can be deceiving* held true in this instance. I'd learned a lot from Wirenut during this morning's surveillance.

A camera mounted on the building's upper-left corner pointed straight at the back door. A novice would avoid the back door and break in the side window because of that camera. Wrong decision. Everything's about illusion in this business. A mere breath, change in temperature, or slight touch on that window would immediately set off the alarm.

"Any other night I'd go in that window," Wirenut whispered. "For the sheer challenge of it."

"Don't get sidetracked," I warned. But I totally understood. Nothing felt more satisfying than cracking a system no one had ever broken. The only difference was I had to have a reason. Wirenut would do it just to do it.

He shook his head. "Not tonight."

Twenty feet of warm night air separated us from the mounted camera. Wirenut pulled out a piece of bamboo. He rolled some putty, pushed it into the end of the bamboo, then peered down the length. He sucked in a breath, held it to his lips, and blew.

The putty whistled through the air and splatted right on the camera lens.

My jaw dropped. Wow. "You need to teach me that."

He grinned.

Pulling our hoods down over our faces, we sprinted from the cemetery through the museum's backyard and halted at the rear door.

Wirenut peeled down the right-index-finger portion of his leather glove. Placing the tip of his finger on the steel door, he closed his eyes and counted.

His eyes shot open. "Water pulse," he whispered.

I blinked. *Water pulse?*

"I didn't expect that. Nobody's *ever* penetrated a water-rigged security system. I've studied all about it. It came out after I joined the Specialists. Otherwise, I would've already tackled it and proven it faulty."

Of course.

"Can you do it?" I had no doubt he could.

He rolled his eyes. "Please. Give me a second."

Slowly, he rubbed his hands together. His gaze focused on nothing in particular as he drifted into deep thought.

"One wrong move, and the entire museum locks down. The building will flood with water stored in oversize pipes in the walls, trapping us and the display pieces. But the display items are protected. We'll drown."

We'll drown? Wait a minute . . .

"Pretty nifty security idea."

I don't think it's too nifty we're going to drown.

"Too bad I'll have to be the first to prove it faulty."

He'd better prove it faulty.

Wirenut reached for his tool pouch. "Okay, think. A building rigged with water will have 1009 proc-gauge wiring. Plastic-coated. It'll be charged by aluminum cantver currents. The water and electricity will flow together, not against each other. Any sort of contact between the two will spark the release. So as long as there's continuous motion of the two, the system will be fooled."

He sounds *like he knows what he's doing.*

"Let's see." He touched the tip of his finger to the door again and held it steady while he counted. He moved it up a fraction, held, counted. He slid it down, held, counted. "A five-second lead interrupts the inch intervals. Which means five-inch segments of black electrical tape, separated by five inches of space, connected by five thicknesses proc-gauge wire will do the trick."

He winked at me. "No problem. What is it with the number five? The crown has five points, too."

"They got a little theme going here."

He took a roll of wire and electrical tape from his vest. He tore off segments of tape, stretched the wire across the door, and then secured the wire at exactly spaced intervals. As he smoothed down the last piece of tape, he gave me a confident nod.

A few seconds later, the door clicked, and Wirenut smiled.

Boy, he's good.

He opened the door, we quickly scooted inside, and it closed behind us with a *click*.

He glanced back. "Wasn't expecting that. Five seconds to get in before everything locks down."

"Good thing we're quick."

He did his victory shoulder-roll dance, and I shook my head at his silliness.

"Okay, don't get too confident. Never know what might happen." Wirenut pressed the talk button on his vest. "We're in."

"Lookout copy," answered TL.

Wirenut took his fiber-lit goggles from his vest. "Let's do this."

In the southwest corner of the one-room museum sat a small wood table. A vault underneath stored the crown at night. According to our research, the crown was pretty much the only thing the museum had. People came from all over the country of Rissala to see it.

We fitted the goggles over our eyes, illuminating the skin-sizzling, yellow lasers.

From my vest I got out the small bottles of chemicals, then flipped open my mini-laptop and keyed the scrambler sequence.

YOU'RE IN, typed Chapling.

HI, I typed back.

From my spot at the back door, I watched Wirenut complete the steps to breaking the Rayver System: leaned at seventy-degree angle, spied tunnel, engaged remote-control expander, wire snaked out and into vault's lock, lasers flicked off, squirted control panel with nitrox, ripped out diversionary wires, red lasers flicked on, found opening tunnel, snipped remaining white one, vault popped open.

Wow, he's quick.

He squatted down, reached inside the vault, and brought out—

A yellow ribbon? What the . . . ?

A ribbon tied around a ruby and a piece of paper. No crown. The burglar had already been here.

Fisting the ruby and paper, Wirenut reared back to slam the vault shut.

"Shhh," I reminded him.

He paused, closed it softly instead, grabbed his tools, and raced back across the tile. The yellow lasers flicked on behind him.

I threw the yellow ribbon aside and took the ruby. "See what the paper says."

Quickly, Wirenut unfolded it. "My boss said to leave this gem behind."

"Is it typed or handwritten?"

"Typed."

"We'll worry about it later." Opening the bottle of barium gentrea, I squeezed out one drop. It glided over the gem. Holding it close, I scrutinized it, studying the chemically bonded numbers as they became visible. Five sets, separated by five spaces with raised edges on every fifth number. Different than the last encrypted message.

"It might disappear on you," Wirenut reminded me.

Like I would forget such a thing. I quickly began keying in the numbers.

"Hurry."

My fingers raced over the keys as I noticed the numbers beginning to disappear.

"Hurry."

My fingers dashed lightning quick to keep up.

"Hurry."

"Got it." I pressed save and made sure Chapling had everything.

The gem went back to normal, appearing as if it hadn't even been touched.

I closed my laptop. "Please don't ever tell me to hurry again. It makes me nervous."

"Sorry."

"That's all right. Let's get out of here."

He did the tape/wire thing to the door, deactivated it, and we slipped out.

▓ ▓ ▓

WIRENUT FLUNG THE YELLOW ribbon and note on the hotel bed. "I can't *believe* he got there before me. I can't *believe* he penetrated the water pulse system." He jabbed his chest.

"*I'm* the one who cracks new systems. Not other people. *I'm* the Ghost."

I didn't think it'd be wise to remind him that technically he was no longer the Ghost. He'd left that behind with his old life when he joined the Specialists.

TL picked up the ribbon. "Sounds like your ego's talking."

Wirenut flopped down on the bed and slung his arm over his eyes. "Leave me alone."

In the months I'd known Wirenut, he'd always maintained a calm, cool demeanor with a spice of humor. I'd seen him irritated and upset more in the past week than I had since first meeting him. It worried me.

This mission was pushing at him from all angles: horrid memories resurfacing about his family, the burglar impersonating him, his meeting Katarina.

All I could do was be a friend, be there for him.

TL picked up the paper. "His boss? He has to be working for Zorba. How else would he know to leave that gem?" TL motioned me to the desk. "Let's see what Chapling's got."

I opened up the laptop. WELL? I typed.

NO GO ON THE DE NUOWSI'T THEOREM, he responded.

"Huh." Slipping on my glasses, I studied the sets of numbers on my screen. "The number five is the theme for this encrypted message. Give me a sec." I took the numbers and rearranged them. Ran them through text identifiers. Cut through user markings. Tagged them defined. Changed the ELD spacing.

Wrapped the preformatted fragment. Deleted fixed processing. Soft-charactered the numerical breaks.

Bingo. "It's code for an image." I ran the code through my vortex imaging program.

OH YEAH. YEAHYEAHYEAH, Chapling typed. SO GOOD.

A 3-D image of a small island appeared. An old mansion occupied pretty much the entire area. The image rotated, and a room appeared. I plugged the coordinates of the island into GPS. "The island is located five towns north of here, five kilometers off shore. I wonder what it is about the number five."

"I was the youngest of five children," Wirenut mumbled from the bed.

I glanced back at him. He still had his arm over his eyes. *Was.* He *was* the youngest of five. How awful to have to say that in the past tense.

TL tapped my knee, and I looked at him. He shook his head slightly, indicating I shouldn't respond to Wirenut.

Pushing my glasses up, I focused back on the laptop. TL was probably right. Wirenut needed to be with his own thoughts right now.

"Cue up the satellite, and let's see what's inside this mansion," TL said.

I pressed a few keys. "According to the original note when the toxin was first stolen, there are three data-encrypted messages. We've retrieved two, so this is the last one. It has to be the sword."

I keyed in the access code to the government's satellite, and through the darkness of midnight, it zeroed in on the mansion. A few more key strokes and it switched to infrared. A couple of clicks and it X-rayed the roof. I zoomed in on the room. "The room is located on the fifth floor, behind the fifth door on the right." I saw an object hanging on the wall and isolated it.

Wirenut sat up and scooted to the edge of the bed.

Beyond the various shades of infrared, a long object became visible.

Wirenut looked over my and TL's shoulders. "Yeah. That's the double-bladed, lion-engraved sword."

The sword his uncle had used.

The laptop bleeped, and Chapling appeared in the lower-left corner. I waved, but he didn't wave back. My stomach clenched with the devastation I saw in his eyes.

Something was wrong. Something was *really* wrong.

TL nodded. "Go ahead."

"New intel. A message came over the line that whoever is looking for the stolen toxin isn't working quickly enough. In two days the toxin will be released. You *have* to get that sword. You *have* to retrieve the last encrypted message. You *have* to find the stolen neurotoxin."

I'd never heard Chapling so adamant.

"We leave at oh eight hundred hours." TL reached for the laptop. "Signing off."

No one said a word as we sat, digesting everything. People

were going to die if we didn't retrieve the last encrypted message. And Wirenut's uncle was behind it all. "How can someone be so sinister?"

"I can't believe I'm related to this man," Wirenut whispered. "Someone told me once that evil is genetic. . . ." His voice trailed off.

The pain in it cracked my heart.

TL gripped the back of Wirenut's neck. "You look at me, and you listen very closely. You wouldn't be a part of the Specialists if you had that kind of blackness in your blood, in your heart. People like your uncle are driven by money and sickness. They get off on watching others suffer. They live to manipulate."

TL let go of Wirenut's neck and grabbed his shoulder. "You are a good man with kindness in your heart that one day will make you a great man." TL released Wirenut. "Now, did you hear everything I said?"

Wirenut closed his eyes. "Yes, sir. Thank you. Excuse me." He crossed the hotel room and walked out the door.

[8]

EARLY THE NEXT MORNING. TL counted Rissalan currency into my hand. "I've reserved a car to take us north of here, then we'll catch a boat over to the island and mansion. The reservation place knows you two are picking it up. Be back here in one hour. I'll meet you out front."

"Yes, sir." I folded the bills and stuffed them in my pants pocket.

Wirenut and I slung our backpacks on and left TL.

As we strolled down the hotel's tile hallway, I cut a quick glance in Wirenut's direction. From the puffiness of his eyes, I'd say he'd had no sleep.

I hadn't seen him since he left his and TL's room last night. I'd gone to mine and crashed. I had no idea what time Wirenut returned or if TL had gone out looking for him.

Looping my arm through Wirenut's, I laid my head on his shoulder. "I love you." I knew he knew I meant sister to brother.

The last time I'd told anyone that, I was six years old, and I'd said it to my parents.

With a sad smile, he kissed my temple. "It's been a long time since I've heard those words."

He was probably afraid to care again. Everyone he'd ever loved had died.

We took the stairs down a flight, crossed the lobby, and exited the hotel. We slipped on sunglasses to cut the early-morning glare and headed up the cobblestone street.

Unzipping my front pocket, I rifled around for my ChapStick and pulled out a lollipop. "I didn't put this in here, did you?"

Wirenut shook his head.

Thinking of you was printed on the stem. *David*. I grinned. "It's from David."

"I see that. And I know you two have been e-mailing each other, so you can stop trying to hide it."

I poked him in the ribs. "You're not supposed to know that."

Smiling, Wirenut looped his arm around my neck. "Come on."

I unwrapped the blueberry lollipop and popped it in my mouth. *Mmmm.*

"Do you mind if we make a quick stop at the café? I told Katarina I'd meet her there. We have time. I want to tell her good-bye. Maybe get her number or something."

I smiled, glad to see his mood lifted. "Sure."

We cut down an alley in the direction of the café and walked in silence. Ahead of us, a red-haired woman opened bright blue shutters. As we passed, I peeked inside. Her children sat around a wood table eating breakfast. A warm, sweet scent floated from their kitchen. The old-world, homey scene brought a contented curve to my lips.

"Let me stop here for a second." He pointed up the alley to where it opened onto a dirt street.

The old, sun-charred jewelry lady, the same one from the marketplace, had spread out her things on a doorstep. She sat on a blanket behind them, creating a new piece.

Wirenut perused her handmade items. He pointed to a gold necklace with an amber stone. "That one. It matches Katarina's eyes."

Aaahhh. I hugged him. He was the best guy ever. Except for David, of course.

Wirenut laughed. "What's that for?"

"Nothing. You're a great guy. That's all."

Ducking his head, he pulled out his wallet. His embarrassed, shy avoidance made me want to hug him again. He paid the lady, took the wrapped necklace, and we continued on our way.

I stuck my lollipop back in my mouth, but I couldn't stop grinning.

He shoved my shoulder. "Stop it. You're ruining my bad-guy image."

We shared a laugh as we rounded the corner to the café.

Katarina stood under the green canvas awning. Behind her, the waitress set the outdoor tables, getting ready for breakfast. No customers had arrived yet.

Katarina watched us approach. She didn't smile or wave or anything. In fact, she didn't seem happy to see us at all.

We stopped beside her and Wirenut slipped off his sunglasses.

"*Jimmu,*" he greeted her softly, as if sensing something wasn't right.

She smoothed her long hair behind her ear. "Hello."

And then nobody said a word. We all just stood in silence, Katarina looking at Wirenut and me and him looking back at her.

Biting her lip, she dropped her gaze to the ground.

Wirenut switched what's-going-on eyes to me.

I shrugged. I had no idea.

He cleared his throat. "Um . . . here." He held out the wrapped necklace. "I bought you something."

She took the small package. "Thank you."

Wirenut clasped her hand. "Katarina, what's going on?"

She swallowed. "My father . . . my father . . ."

Oh, God, no. Had her father died?

"My father saw us together at the marketplace yesterday and got really mad. I'm sorry." A tear slid down her cheek. "He doesn't want me to see you again."

▦ ▦ ▦

IN SILENCE. WE CONTINUED on to pick up the rental car, then TL, and now here I sat, idly staring out the open passenger window as TL drove up the coast to our destination. Warm, salty air flowed through the car, through my body, relaxing me a little. Clear aqua water spanned to eternity on my right, and jagged cliffs boxed us in on the left. I'd never been one to sit and "smell the roses," as they say, but this part of Rissala was definitely the most beautiful place I'd ever seen.

Wirenut sat in the backseat studying the mansion's schematics and the private island the mansion occupied.

He hadn't said a word about Katarina. He had to be thinking about her, though. I'd asked him a few hours ago if he was okay. He'd simply nodded and continued analyzing the blueprints. I supposed it was good he had something to occupy his brain.

"Okay," Wirenut called over the wind. "I'm ready."

We rolled up our windows, and TL cranked on the air. I turned in my seat to listen.

Wirenut tapped his legal pad. "This mansion's locked down tight. But I've figured it out. There's an invisible fence surrounding the private island. The fence is located in the water. The only way in is to swim under it."

TL adjusted the rearview mirror. "How far down?"

"Hundred feet."

A hundred feet? I'd had only a couple of diving lessons back at the ranch as part of our PT. But that'd been in a twenty-five-foot-deep pool. *A hundred feet?* That was *really* far down.

"You'll do fine," TL reassured me, as if sensing my wandering, I'm-starting-to-freak-out thoughts.

"There's only one location we can swim under," Wirenut continued. "The opening is located on the west side, fifty feet off the island's shore. Once we're through the invisible fence, we have to scale the east wall of the mansion. There're only five windows on the east side. We'll have to climb between the fourth and fifth windows. Once we're on the roof, we'll rappel down through the fifth chimney into the mansion. According to the X-rayed image GiGi pulled up last night, we'll be in the room where the sword is located."

Wow. As always, very thorough.

TL turned off the coastal highway onto a dirt road. "Good work."

"One last thing." Wirenut pressed the off button on his hand-held, electronic schematics. "With this particular security setup, one misstep rigs the mansion to explode."

Explode?

▦ ▦ ▦

Hours Later, TL pulled into a marina parking lot. "Whatever I say or do, you two play along with it."

Wirenut and I nodded.

I held up my finger. "Can we talk about the exploding thing again?"

Both guys sighed. "GiGi, you'll do fine."

They'd said that about a zillion times since Wirenut mentioned it. Their not-this-again, chorused answer made me smile. They knew me too well.

TL slid the keys from the ignition. "Give GiGi and me a second."

With a nod, Wirenut exited the car.

TL turned to me. "Under no circumstances do you show any recognition of the person we're about to see. Understand?"

"Who are we about to see?"

"Do you understand?"

I *hated* when he didn't answer my questions. "Yes, sir."

TL opened his door and climbed out. "Get your stuff, kids. It's going to be a *fuuun* day."

Kids?

Beside us a couple with twin boys pulled towels, fishing rods, duffel bags, and other vacationy things from their car. Other than them and us, the marina parking lot sat empty.

TL popped the trunk. He handed a cooler to Wirenut. "Carry that. We got some yummy munchies in there."

When had we gotten a cooler? And "yummy munchies"? TL would never in a million years say "yummy munchies."

Wirenut must have thought so, too, because he laughed.

TL ruffled Wirenut's hair. "Whatcha laughing at, sport? It's going to be a *beee-uuu-ti-ful* day." He tossed a couple of backpacks at me. "Carry those for me, girlie girl."

Sport? Girlie girl? I tried not to laugh.

Slinging diving bags over his shoulder, TL slammed the trunk. "Glory *be*, it's magnificent here. Maybe we'll see some of those *enooormous* stingrays."

He led the way across the marina parking lot and onto a wooden path. Trees bordered both sides and opened to a rocky beach. The path led to a dock that stretched out over the water.

TL pointed off to the right. "Look at that water. Have you *ever* seen *anything* so gorgeous in your life?"

Wirenut cut a quick glance in my direction, and we shared a smile. TL was never this talkative or happy.

"Well, have you?"

"No," Wirenut quickly responded. "Never have."

We came to the end of the dock, where a rickety wooden boat floated, tied off. Behind us, the parking-lot family boarded a safer-looking one.

TL sat his dive bags down. "Here we go. Doesn't look like much. But we're going to have *tooons* of fun."

Shielding my eyes from the early-afternoon sun, I surveyed the twenty-five-foot weather-beaten boat. It didn't appear as if it could float, much less take us safely five kilometers to the private island and mansion.

A crash-bang echoed from the small pilothouse, followed by a string of curses. Dressed in filthy overalls, a woman stumbled out, rubbing her ball-cap-covered head.

She snorted, hacked her throat, and spit.

Nasty.

She took off her cap. Long, greasy, black hair fell down her back. Scratching her scalp, she looked up at the three of us and stretched her lips into a toothless grin.

I froze. *Nalani?*

What was TL's wife doing here? The last time I'd seen her, we'd been in Ushbania running for our lives. She hadn't looked anything like she did now. She'd had teeth. And manners. And clean hair. She'd been beautiful.

Nalani put her cap back on. "Welcome aboard, maties. *Mi casa es su casa.*" She snorted a laugh. "That's Spanish, not Rissalan."

TL tossed her the dive bags. "We're *sooo* excited. My name's Tim. That's Stan holding the cooler and Dana with the backpacks."

Wirenut and I waved. Well, I waved. Wirenut nodded because of the cooler. I tried to catch Nalani's eye, but she was completely in role. A stranger to us. Someone we'd hired for the day.

Nalani saluted. "Call me captain. Now get on board. Times a wastin'. We're shoving off in one minute."

She disappeared into the pilothouse. The engine sputtered to life a second later. We loaded our things, untied the boat, and motored away from the dock.

I stood beside Wirenut, watching the rocky beach disappear until only water surrounded us. An unsettled feeling weighed down my stomach, and I thought back all those years to the plane crash I'd been in with my parents. All the water. Swimming. Crying for them . . .

Sighing at the memory, I glanced over my shoulder to the pilothouse. TL stood just inside the door, staring at Nalani's back as she drove the boat. My heart ached for him. For both of them. It had in Ushbania, too. Their covers prohibited them from interacting like a couple.

He took a step into the pilothouse, peering over her shoulder. His fingers trailed across her lower back as he pretended interest in the boat's control panel. He shifted a little closer, and, although I couldn't see real well, I thought he kissed her on the neck.

I wondered, as I had before, why they weren't together. Why didn't she live at the ranch with us? Why did they even get married?

For hours we zigzagged the coast, pretending to sightsee, each time getting a little closer to the private island. Anyone who might be watching, listening, or have us on radar would assume we were just another group of tourists.

Sitting in the distance, the small island stretched about a half mile long and a quarter mile wide. The centuries-old stone mansion occupied roughly half the island. It stood dark and spooky on the horizon. According to my research, no one lived in the mansion. It was owned by the country of Rissala and rented out for special occasions.

Not that stolen neurotoxin was considered a special occasion.

The sun slipped into darkness. Nalani cut the engine and dropped the anchor.

Wirenut handed me an apple and a cheese sandwich. "Eat this. We've got a long night ahead of us." He sat down beside me, dangling his feet over the side of the boat. "The captain works for us, doesn't she?"

Biting into my apple, I shrugged. In Ushbania I'd been the only one who didn't know Nalani was on our side. I hadn't suspected anything and didn't find out until the very end that she was one of us.

Silly to admit, but I liked being in the know this time around.

Clearly, though, Wirenut was more perceptive than me.

We finished our food and continued sitting, patiently waiting, staring at the dark water until TL touched our backs.

He tapped two fingers to his left shoulder. *Time to go.*

Behind him, Nalani opened the cooler, revealing equipment piled inside. She handed Wirenut and me black Velcro belts. "Tool belt. Strap these to your thighs so they're hidden."

Leaning in, Wirenut smiled. "I knew she worked for us," he whispered.

⠿ ⠿ ⠿

IΠ ΟUΓ WΞT SUITS. we flutter-kicked our way through the dark ocean. Wirenut first, me second, and TL brought up the rear.

With our rebreathers, no bubbles trailed upward. Water plugged my ears, permitting me to hear only my heartbeat and slow deep breaths.

Wirenut extended his arms out to his sides, indicating in ten seconds we would pass through the opening in the invisible fence.

Through my night goggles, I kept my vision focused on Wirenut's fins. *One misstep rigs the mansion to explode.*

Talk about pressure.

We made it through the fence and continued underwater around the island to the east side. The sandy ocean floor rose gradually until we swam in only ten feet of depth. Our slow ascent decompressed our bodies.

We exited the water and stripped our diving gear, then piled it on the sliver of rocky beach.

Still in our wet suits, we jogged over the flat rocks to the mansion's east wall. Between the fourth and fifth windows, Wirenut gazed up five stories to the roof. He leaned to the right a little and tilted his head.

He placed his ear against the wall, moved a few feet to the left and listened there, then went back to his original spot. From his vest he pulled four pressurized suction cups. Two he strapped to his knees and two he held in his hands. TL and I did the same. Air release controlled the suction, allowing for silent attachment and release. They worked on any surface.

Wirenut turned to us, touched his eye, and held up one finger. *Watch closely. One at a time.*

TL and I nodded. Wirenut suctioned onto the stone and began a spiderlike crawl. Left arm, left leg. Right arm, right leg. I scrutinized his form, memorizing his technique and rhythm. At the third story he scooted to the right and continued crawling. At the fifth story he moved back to his original spot.

He made it to the roof and signaled for me.

One misstep rigs the mansion to explode.

With a deep breath I suctioned onto the wall.

9

TRYING TO BE A SPIDER crawling up five stories of stone was *not* as easy as Wirenut made it look.

A week after my Ushbanian mission, I'd seen him using these suction cups at the ranch. I'd played around with them on the side of our two-story, wooden barn, more for fun than anything. But that time wasn't anything like right now.

Wood versus stone. Big difference.

Two stories versus five. Another big difference.

You'd think I'd have learned by now to expect the unexpected. Maybe years into this secret-agent thing, I'd be so experienced nothing would faze me.

Like TL.

At the third story I stopped to catch my breath. Shutting my eyes, I inhaled the musty scent of stone and blew out slowly through my mouth. Again in deeply through my nose and out my mouth. Like TL had taught me.

Gradually, my thumping heart stilled to a normal putter. Only two more stories to go.

Bruiser would have no problem scaling this wall. She'd already be on the roof doing back flips or some such thing.

I opened my eyes to moldy, moist stone. Ignoring my shaky, fatigued muscles, I used my thumb to depress the button on my right suction cup. A tiny puff of air indicated that the seal was broken. I moved my hand farther up the wall and reattached.

I scooted to the right like I'd seen Wirenut do and then back to the left at the fifth story. Mere feet from the roof, I stopped, my breath rushing in and out, and tilted my head back. My entire body screamed with exertion as I met Wirenut's eyes.

He lay belly down on the mansion's roof, his hand stretching out toward me. I inched a little farther up, and he latched onto my forearm.

Oh, thank God. I'd thought I was in better shape.

With a stifled grunt, he tugged me onto the roof, and I rolled onto my back, gasping for air.

"Shhh," he reminded me.

Staring at the night sky, I focused on the half moon and concentrated on steadying my breath and heart.

Exhale.

Inhale.

Exhale.

Inhale.

TL quietly stepped up beside me, breathing normally. As if he'd gone for a leisurely stroll in the park.

I definitely needed more physical training.

Never thought I'd actually think those words.

Swallowing to moisten my dehydrated mouth, I got to my feet and looked around.

Fat brick chimneys dotted the roof. A dozen of them. This mansion must have a lot of fireplaces.

Wirenut stood beside one about three feet tall, looping rappelling wire around a protruding brick. I scanned the haphazardly placed chimneys, wondering how he knew that was the fifth one.

He signaled us, and we wove through the maze to him. Wirenut climbed up and disappeared over the edge. I peeked past the bricks and watched him slip into the darkness.

Well, this is something new. I'd never rappelled. TL had gone over the procedures in the car on the drive up the coast. But as I mentioned earlier, real life *never* mirrored simulation.

It was impossible to prepare completely for every single situation. I was such a novice, thrown into these missions quite unexpectedly. Eventually, I'd have the skills needed.

TL touched my shoulder and then tapped his watch. *Go.*

He had faith in me, so that had to count for something. I did do all right on the Ushbanian mission. Well, aside from a few mishaps.

I slipped on night-vision goggles, climbed up the chimney, and attached hand grips to the rappelling wire like TL had told me to. Folding my legs around it, I slowly slid down the passage. The cushioned hand grips did most of the work. I just had to hold on. For once, something physical came easy for me.

Through my goggles, I made out gray shades of bricks and cobwebs. No spiders. This passage had to be at least six feet wide. I hadn't imagined chimneys would be so roomy.

About twenty feet later I landed with a soft thud on the fire grate. No ashes. No coals. No wood. No signs that a fire had ever been built.

Squatting down, I stepped from the oversized opening into an empty room. No furniture. No decorations. Nothing.

Wirenut stood in the center of the room staring at a spot above me. I turned. The double-bladed lion-engraved sword hung right above the fireplace, a few feet from my head.

The sword Wirenut's uncle had used to kill his entire family.

The sword holding the final message that would lead to the stolen neurotoxin.

TL stepped from the fireplace and immediately looked up to see what Wirenut and I stared at.

"Don't," Wirenut mumbled, "touch it."

TL and I turned back to Wirenut.

He pointed to the row of marble tile leading straight toward him. "Come to me. Do not step off the tile."

One misstep rigs the mansion to explode.

I went first down the row of foot-wide tile, and TL followed. We met Wirenut in the middle.

Wirenut tapped his fiber-lit goggles. "I can tell that this," he indicated the circular change in marble pattern about five feet in diameter, "is the safe zone. Do not step from it. As soon as I start working, that tile you walked down won't be available. It'll be covered with lasers."

TL replaced his night-vision goggles with fiber-lit ones. "Put yours on."

I followed his instructions. Yellow lasers flicked into view, completely filling the room, zigzagging inches from our circular safe zone and the path we'd come down.

Jeez, and to think if I'd lost my step I would've been fried.

A blue glow enveloped the sword. As Wirenut contemplated it, I took the mini-laptop from my vest.

"Son of a—" he breathed. "We activated that when we came down the fireplace."

"What is it?" TL asked.

"It's a pulse bomb. Incinerates anything with a heartbeat."

My whole body jerked to attention. "That means . . . that means . . ." I swallowed. I knew about pulse bombs. They were the most lethal ones on the market. "That means every human and animal within two hundred miles will be a pile of ashes if we trigger it."

Wirenut nodded.

TL cupped Wirenut's shoulder. "You can do this. Don't focus on the pulse bomb. Concentrate on doing what you do best, and we'll make it out alive."

TL turned to me. "Don't you think about it either. Get the laptop ready. Focus."

I barely heard him over my hammering heart.

"Both of you, we've made it this far knowing the mansion could explode. This pulse bomb is just another obstacle. Let's do it."

Yeah, but everyone within two hundred miles? That meant people back in the capital city, Katarina, Nalani—

Suddenly, the door to the room opened. We whipped our

heads around to the right. The burglar, the imposter Ghost, stood in the threshold. One step inside and the lasers would fry him.

"You don't want to do this. Not now." Wirenut indicated the sword. "That's a pulse bomb."

"I know." The burglar pointed a tiny silver disc at the sword. He pressed the top of the disc, and the blue glow went out. "Pulse bomb's not a problem anymore. I'm here for the sword."

Something digitized his voice, masking its real sound, just like before.

"What is that?" Wirenut asked. "Where did you get that?"

The burglar slipped the disc inside his vest. "You're not the only one gifted in the homemade-electronic-contraption department."

"B-but . . ."

"What? Don't like being shown up?"

"Ignore him," TL whispered. "Focus on the sword. We'll get him later."

"Oh, and one last thing." The burglar slipped another object from his vest. A slim black square.

He pointed it at each corner of the room. On the last corner, the yellow lasers flicked out. Pink ones immediately took their place, zigzagging everywhere but the circular safe zone, the area in front of the fireplace, and the entrance to the room.

The burglar stepped inside and closed the door behind him.

Wirenut sighed. "Great."

I shifted. "What is it?"

"Contortion lasers. Named that because you have to be a freakin' gymnast to get through them." Wirenut took off his vest, leaving him dressed in only his wet suit, hood, and goggles. "No equipment needed. Just like the others, they'll definitely fry you."

The burglar took off his vest, too. He slid to a split, grasped his left calf, and flattened his upper body along the length of his leg. He rolled under a laser not more than eight inches from the floor.

I cringed. *That* had to hurt.

Extending his arms above his head, Wirenut leapt up and dove through a laser opening about six feet off the ground. He landed on the other side.

I caught my breath. *Wow.*

Still in a split, the burglar tilted his body a tiny bit. He curved his left leg forward, his right leg back, and lifted up with his hands. Hovering a few inches from the tile, he rotated like a slow-motion windmill through the crisscrossed lasers.

I blinked. *This guy's good.*

From his handstand position, Wirenut lowered himself inch by inch, bowing backward, slinking beneath a laser. Halfway under he paused, tucked in his left arm, and balanced his entire body on his right hand. Carefully, he crept the rest of the way, using only his fingers to crawl forward.

My jaw dropped. I had no idea Wirenut was that strong.

The burglar stood pencil straight. Lasers zigzagged all around him, literally a millimeter's width from frying him. I scrutinized him and the lasers and couldn't see an opening anywhere.

In a flash, he moved. Jumping, spinning, flipping. Landing in a tight little ball. He flinched and hissed in a breath. His black bodysuit spread open on his lower back. A thin stream of blood trickled out. One of the lasers had gotten him.

I gritted my teeth. *Ow.*

Squatted down, Wirenut swept his left leg around. He pushed up, spun, and caught air on a scissors kick, then corkscrewed through a diamond-shaped opening.

I smiled. *Bruiser would be so proud.*

The burglar shot forward at an angle, shoved off the wall with his boots, and back-flipped to the fireplace. Right in front of the sword.

I snapped my focus to Wirenut.

One single wall of interwoven lasers separated him from the other guy and the sword. The burglar straightened; he pulled his shoulders back in a lazy stretch, obviously showing off the fact he'd made it to the fireplace first.

Wirenut thrust his arm through an opening, gripped the burglar's throat, and yanked him forward. The burglar went very still, barely breathing.

With dozens of skin-sizzling lasers between them, Wirenut held the burglar inches from his face. "Who are you? What do you want?"

The burglar didn't respond.

"Why are you imitating me?"

No response.

"Do you work for Zorba?"

No response.

Wirenut pulled him a threatening fraction closer, and my stomach contracted.

"No," TL commanded. "Do not harm him."

Wirenut reached through with his other hand and ripped away the burglar's hood.

I gasped. *Katarina?*

All the zigzagging lasers flicked off. Immediately, a green glow encompassed the two of them, trapping them together.

A door hidden in the wall slid open, and a tall, olive-skinned man dressed in a white suit stepped out.

He bowed, all proper. "Good evening. I am Octavias Zorba. So nice of everyone to come."

Oh, my God. Wirenut's uncle.

I shot a quick glance at Wirenut. He stood frozen, staring through the green glow at his uncle.

Octavias tapped his black cane to the floor, pleasantly stern. "Now, let's see who everyone is. Remove your hoods."

I looked at TL. He didn't acknowledge me, just kept his focus level on Mr. Zorba.

Seconds rolled by, and nobody moved.

Octavias sighed, dramatically put out. "All right then. If you insist." He pointed his cane at TL. "This button right here," he tapped the silver handle, "will activate the paralysis cathode."

Oh, crap. A paralysis cathode could be dialed to severity, either rendering someone unconscious or paralyzed for seconds or putting him in a coma for days.

Octavias pressed the button.

TL dropped to the ground.

I sucked in a breath. "T-TL."

I scrambled the few feet to him, fumbled with his wet suit and hood, searching for his neck and a pulse.

TL's eyes flew open, and I jumped back.

With obvious discomfort, he sat up. "Do what he says," he rasped.

He took his hood off, and we followed his lead.

"Stan?" Katarina whispered.

They stared into each other's eyes, not moving, confusion and betrayal evident in both their faces. My heart broke for the two of them.

Wirenut looked at her. "You . . ."

She didn't answer, just dropped her head in shame.

Octavias tapped his cane. "Do it." His tone wasn't so pleasant now.

Katarina shook her head.

"I said," he barely moved his lips, "do it."

She lifted a distressed gaze to Octavias. "I can't, Papa. I know him."

Papa?

What the . . . ?

That meant Wirenut and Katarina were cousins?

Octavias pointed his cane at me, and my heart nearly stopped. "Do it."

Do what? Somebody do something. I don't want that thing pointed at me.

With a worried, indecisive glance my way, Katarina tenderly cradled Wirenut's face in her hands.

"I'm so sorry," she murmured, a tear slipping down her cheek.

She went up on her tiptoes and softly pressed her lips to his.

The green glow dissipated, and Katarina stepped away.

Groaning through a grimace, Wirenut hunched forward, gripping his stomach. Seconds later he slumped to his knees. TL and I moved, and Octavias shook his cane, emphasizing he still had it pointed at us.

Helplessly, we watched Wirenut. Quivers began to spasm his body, little jerks, as though somebody were shocking him.

Or had poisoned him.

The kiss.

I glared at Katarina. "What did you do?"

She peeled a clear film from her lips. "Arsenic mouth tape."

My stomach dropped.

Katarina avoided my gaze. "It won't kill him."

"How could you?" I said, staring at her.

She raced across the room and disappeared through the door Octavias had come from.

Wirenut fell to his side. Foamy spit seeped out of his mouth as his spasming body morphed into an all-out seizure.

"Stop it!" I screamed at Octavias.

He sneered.

Lifting his cane, he pressed a button, and the tile opened beneath me.

I sailed into darkness.

10

SLOWLY. CAREFULLY. I opened my eyes, cringing from the invasion of a little light into my skull.

My entire head throbbed, like someone had crawled inside it and banged my brain with a sledgehammer.

Shutting my eyes, I didn't move, allowing myself to regain consciousness naturally. Like TL had taught me to.

Hone in on your senses, he'd told me.

I focused on taste first, moving my tongue around my mouth. Dry. A little puffy. Other than an obvious need for water, nothing out of the ordinary.

I moved to my nose next, inhaling. My nostrils flared at the subtle scent of incense burning somewhere.

I switched to my ears. Silence. No, wait . . . breathing. Someone else was breathing.

My head lifted . . . then fell.

Lifted . . . then fell.

I'm lying on someone's stomach, I realized, as my head lifted again with the sound of the breath.

I opened my eyes again, relieved the sledgehammer in my brain had eased.

Above me stretched a wood ceiling. Shadows played across it in the dimly lit room, as though a candle flickered nearby. Maybe the incense was really scented wax.

My arms were beneath me. My legs stretched out and crossed at the ankles. I tried a tiny movement and failed.

Tied. Just as I expected.

I wiggled my numb, cool fingers and twisted my wrists. It felt like metal ties bound me, not rope or tape. A chain maybe? Or steel band?

"Stay still," a voice spoke.

TL. I breathed a sigh of contentment. Amazing how much a familiar, trusted voice can calm you.

"You took a hard hit to the head when you fell."

"Guess that explains the sledgehammer in my brain."

He chuckled, and my head bounced (*ow*) with his stomach's movement. At least I knew whose belly I was on now.

I moved my tongue around, trying to work up saliva. "Where are we?"

"Somewhere in the mansion."

"Are you tied up?"

"Yes. Different than you, though. I'm shackled to the floor. I haven't figured it out yet, but I'm certain we're booby-trapped."

I rolled my head and eyes just enough to the left to see his face. "Can I get up?"

"Try. Carefully."

Slowly rotating toward him, I smooshed my face into his

side, using it for leverage to push myself to my knees.

Suddenly, the chains began to crank. TL groaned.

"Oh, my God. Did I do that?" The release of my weight must have triggered the booby trap.

They clanked to a stop.

"It's okay," he breathed.

Still dressed in his wet suit, TL lay spread-eagled on the cement. Chains coming from holes in the floor restrained each arm and leg separately, pulling them tight, like a medieval torturing device.

I looked up then, straight into Wirenut's eyes, and sucked in a breath.

Like TL, Wirenut was shackled spread-eagle. But to the wall instead of the floor. He stared wide-eyed, unblinking, into space. His relaxed mouth and unfocused gaze told me he lacked consciousness. His expanding and contracting chest proved he was breathing.

Thank God.

I looked down at TL. "What happened?"

"Right after you dropped through the floor, Zorba hit me with the paralysis cathode again. I woke up here, chained, Wirenut on the wall, you on my stomach."

"How long have we been here?"

Lifting his head, TL nodded across the room. "Clock on the wall."

It read five. We'd entered the mansion at one in the morning.

We'd been here four hours. And the two people I counted on the most were locked up with me. The only chance of rescue was . . . "Nalani?"

"GiGi," TL sighed. "There's nothing she can do. This mansion is locked down tight. You know that. You saw what we went through to get in. If it weren't for Wirenut, we *wouldn't* have gotten in. She's not coming. She's waiting for us on the boat where she dropped us."

I squeezed my eyes closed as the realization of our situation hit me hard. Wirenut chained. TL chained. Me bound.

No one's coming. *No one's coming.*

Fear rocked my body, and my muscles tensed.

We're going to die.

"GiGi," TL snapped, and my eyes shot open.

He pierced me with one of his lethal glares. "We do not have time for you to get scared. You have to focus. You're the only one mobile. Do you understand?"

I jerked my head into a nod.

"Now shift your legs, flex your muscles, see if your tool belt is still strapped to your thigh."

Blowing out a shaky breath, I did as TL said. "Yes."

"Good." TL nodded. "Now that you're awake, you've got a better view than me. Describe the room."

I glanced around, consciously forcing my fear aside. "About a forty-by-twenty rectangle. Brick walls. Cement floor. Wood-beam ceiling. Two-foot-tall candle lit in each corner, encased by an urn." I nodded to my right. "That wall is covered with photos and newspaper clippings."

TL rolled his head back to see. "Photos of what?"

I squinted. "Can't tell."

"Move closer. Cautiously. Stop as soon as you can make it out."

With my eyes glued to the wall, I scooted my knees over the cement. Right, then left. Right, then left. Inch by inch I shuffled away from TL and across the room.

I stopped and sucked in a breath. My eyes bounced from one picture to the next. "They're all of Wirenut. At different ages. Everything from a baby to a boy to now." *How weird.*

"Are they posed?"

"No. They're candid snapshots of everyday life. Walking into a home, playing on a swing, coming out of school. Pictures of houses, buildings, and other people, too."

"Looks like Zorba's been keeping up with his nephew."

"Yeah, this place is like a shrine."

"What are the newspaper clippings?"

I squinted, studied each one. "They're about the Ghost. I'd say there's three dozen. From all over the world." Wirenut had international fame. "Guess Zorba knows Wirenut and the Ghost are one and the same."

Wirenut moaned, and I jerked around. His eyelids dropped. Groggily, he tried to move.

"Stay still," TL instructed. "You're alive. GiGi and I are right here with you. You're chained up. Don't fight it. Focus on your surroundings. Block the . . ."

While TL continued calmly coaching Wirenut to consciousness, I knee-shuffled back across the room.

Wirenut opened his eyes and looked straight at me.

I smiled a little. I didn't think I'd ever been so relieved to see another person awake in my entire life.

He tried to smile back, but it came out as more of a lip twitch. He looked so exhausted I wanted to hug him.

He licked his lips. "Where are we?" he slurred.

TL relayed everything he had said to me.

I pointed with my head toward the picture wall. "Your uncle's been keeping up with you."

While Wirenut studied the wall, I described to him what I had seen.

When I was done, he sighed. "What does he want with me?"

"We'll find out soon enough." TL lifted his head. "Look around the room. Tell me what you think."

Wirenut took a minute, studying the walls, corners, ceiling, floor, chains. It seemed as though he didn't leave a single inch unscrutinized.

"Turn around, GiGi. Let me see what Zorba put on you."

I did.

Wirenut nodded. "These chains make it look old world. But it's not. At all. Motion sensors in each corner. When triggered the chains crank tighter. The room's divided into small zones.

Certain spots will activate my restraints. Other spots TL's. And yet others, both of ours."

"What's the trigger?" asked TL.

"The steel bands around GiGi's wrists."

What? "Me? I'm the trigger?"

Wirenut nodded.

TL tugged on his holds. "So my movement's okay?"

"Yes." Wirenut moved. "Mine, too."

I twisted my wrists. "Then all we have to do is get my bands off?"

"That's right."

I glanced around. "And a door? How do we get out of this place?"

Wirenut indicated the picture wall. "Hidden door's there. The release of all of our bonds will trigger it to open."

Before TL or I could respond, a portion of the picture wall soundlessly slid open. Octavias Zorba stepped through the opening. Before the doorway glided closed, I saw that a dark tunnel stretched behind him.

I scooted closer to TL. Not that he could protect me or anything. But being near him made me feel safe.

"I see that everyone's awake. Good." Zorba lifted his cane and pointed it at Wirenut.

"No!" I screamed. Hadn't he been through enough?

Zorba shot me a condescending, amused glance. "Dear, your concern touches me."

I clenched my jaw. I wanted to rip off his face.

He pressed a button on the cane, and a panel next to Wirenut's head slid open.

Whistling, twirling his cane, Zorba strolled across the room.

If we could get that cane, we'd be home free. It seemed to control everything in this mansion.

Unmoving, Wirenut watched as his uncle got closer and closer. I could only imagine what horrid scenes raced through Wirenut's brain, staring into the eyes of the man who slaughtered his entire family.

Zorba stopped only an inch away. Wirenut didn't look away and, in fact, lifted his chin a notch.

I was so proud of him for not being intimidated. Or at least not showing it if he felt it.

Zorba reached into the panel and pulled out the double-bladed, lion-engraved sword. Two shiny, silver blades extended from a black handle. A red lion had been etched into each long, sharp edge. A small space separated the twin blades. If a person was stabbed, they'd have two puncture wounds instead of one.

The fierce reality of the weapon stunned me.

Slowly, Zorba brought it down, trailing it across Wirenut's chest. Taunting him.

Wirenut swallowed, but made no other movement.

Zorba twirled away, wielding the sword and the cane, slashing them through the air.

I stared at Wirenut, hoping he'd look at me, willing him all the emotional support I could. He wouldn't take his eyes off his uncle, though.

Zorba tapped the picture wall with the sword. "As you can see, I've kept tabs on you. I knew you'd turn out to be great. I saw the possibilities in you even when you were a baby. That's why I saved you, you know? Because you were gifted. The rest of your family"—Zorba flicked his wrist—"useless. All of them. Especially your father, my *big* brother. I hated him. I always hated him. And your mother? We were engaged. Did you know that? She used to be mine, until my *big* brother met her."

His venomous words spoken in a nonchalant, whatever tone brought tears to my eyes. *He'd massacred Wirenut's family because they were useless?*

"And actually, I told your father I'd kill his family if he went to the police about all my business dealings. Guess he didn't believe me." Zorba sauntered over to one of the urns. "I'm a man of my word." He stroked the blade through the flame of the candle that sat in the corner. "I lost track of you after the New Mexico arrest. Where you first met my precious Katarina."

He slid the cane into a side holster on his hip. "I set all this up, you know? Katarina impersonating the Ghost. The neuro-toxin. It was all to test you. To flush you out. Turns out I flushed out a few people with you. But don't worry, I'll take care of them when I'm ready."

He turned from the candle. "So look at me. I'm brilliant. Because here you are."

"What do you want with me?" Wirenut asked.

"Why, nephew, I'm surprised by your query. I want you to come work for me, of course."

"Never."

Zorba slid his finger over one of the sword's tips, bringing blood. "You're probably wondering why I didn't just keep you. Raise you myself." His cordial tone turned menacing. "Kind of hard to do with being arrested, getting a new identity. And you got lost in the system there for a while, too. Turns out it worked better to watch you from a distance. To see where your gifts lie. Unfortunately, I think I should've taken you sooner. Seems this organization you work for has brought out too much goodness in you. Time to get you back." Zorba stroked his bloody finger down one cheek and then the other.

Wirenut's chains rattled, jerking my attention away from Zorba. Wide-eyed, shaking, Wirenut stared at his uncle, seeming hypnotized by him.

The bone-deep fear sent a chill through my body.

Zorba trailed blood across his forehead. "Look familiar?"

Wirenut gasped for a breath. And then another.

This was probably what Zorba had done right before butchering Wirenut's family. Some sort of ritual.

Which meant Zorba planned on doing the same . . . to us.

TL rotated his wrist in a steady, repetitive pattern. *Clickclack. Clickclack. Clickclack.*

The soft clinking of his chains drew my frantic thoughts. I focused hard on his bound wrist and seconds later looked into his eyes. The assured calmness in their depths brought me peace and confidence. I knew what TL was doing. He'd told me once that making a repetitive noise would calm a nervous teammate.

"Good, GiGi. Now Wirenut," TL whispered. "Let's get him focused and under control."

In unison we *clickclacked*. TL with his chains and me tapping my nail to the steel band around my wrists. Little by little, Wirenut's body stopped shaking. He dragged his eyes from his uncle and focused on us.

Mentally, I transmitted all the confidence I felt.

We're going to be okay.

Seconds later his expression softened, and I knew he felt it, too.

Zorba turned and pointed the sword at me. "Tell me, dear, where do your talents lie?"

I glanced down at TL, and he nodded.

"Computers," I answered. "Code."

"Oh, yes. Can't have a team without a computer genius." Leisurely, he crossed the short distance between us, stopping at TL's head.

Zorba loved being in control, toying with a person's psyche. He reveled in it. It was written all over his face.

He put the sword tip down next to TL's ear. "I'll assume you're the man in charge. Tell me, man in charge, how did you go about getting such talented kids? I'll bet you have a whole group of them somewhere."

TL shrugged. "Not that I know of."

Zorba teetered the sword back and forth. "Don't suppose you'd be in the mood to do a little swap. Your life for the location of your special kids?"

TL didn't take his eyes off Zorba. "No deal."

"I'll pay."

"No thanks."

"All right then." Zorba flicked his wrist, and TL stiffened. Blood flew across the room.

"You bastard!" I screamed.

Zorba snickered at my outburst.

I glanced down at TL. I couldn't see exactly where he'd been cut, but it looked like his ear.

Zorba whistled his way over to Wirenut. "Let's see if my little nephew still has his scars. He tried to save his family, you know? He jumped on my back and tried to choke me." Zorba clucked his tongue. "Silly five-year-old boy."

Zorba trailed the sword from Wirenut's shoulder across his chest down to his hip. Then did the other side, tracing a giant X on Wirenut's body.

Wirenut kept his attention fastened on TL. Good thing, because he wouldn't see calmness in my eyes. He'd see downright pissed-offness.

"Leave him alone," I warned, anger boiling in my veins.

Zorba cut me another one of those condescending, amused glances. "Or what?"

I tightened my jaw.

He peeled Wirenut's wet suit away, revealing his entire upper body. Wirenut flinched. A long, jagged scar bisected his shoulder.

The gruesomeness of it morphed my boiling anger into full-on rage.

Way back in the crevices of my subconscious, I felt TL's eyes on me. But my fury made me ignore him.

Zorba tapped Wirenut's scar with the sword. "Scars make great conversation pieces. I think it healed quite nicely."

Wirenut's breath quickened. His stomach contracted. And I went over the edge.

With my bound ankles and wrists, I propelled my body weight headfirst over TL, dropped to a roll, and swung my feet out.

Zorba tripped to the ground.

Chains clanked. I'd triggered my teammates' torturous restraints.

One of them groaned.

I blocked my need to help them and focused on Zorba instead.

I tumbled toward him just as he pushed up, brought my feet back, and rammed them into his crotch.

He dropped to his knees with a grunt.

I swung around to my back and crammed my heels into his throat.

He gagged.

I swerved to my knees, grabbed the cane with my mouth, and ripped it from his side holster.

Immediately, I tasted blood.

Chains cranked. TL and Wirenut groaned.

With the cane clenched between my teeth, I slid away. I put it on the ground pointing toward Zorba, and, with my nose, I mashed the button I'd seen him press.

The paralysis cathode.

Zorba thunked to the floor.

"The red button!" Wirenut shouted over his pain.

I ground my nose into the red button. The chains halted. My heart stopped.

I looked at TL, stretched to the limit, gritting his teeth against the pain. Blood from his injury pooled under his head.

"What do I do?"

"Get your tool belt," Wirenut hissed.

Get my tool belt? It was still strapped to my thigh.

I hobbled up beside Zorba and lay down next to the sword. I slid my thigh along one of the blades to cut it from my leg. Instead, the blade nicked my skin, and I cringed. My wet suit split open.

"Hurry!" Wirenut yelled. "He's waking up."

I glanced up, right into Zorba's eyes.

zorba's black eyes narrowed to two tiny slits.

Not giving him a chance to think, move, or even breathe, I used my knees to ram the sword in his direction.

He roared in pain as blood squirted my face.

"The cane!" Wirenut yelled.

I rolled away from Zorba over to the cane, squirmed my body toward the handle, and crammed my nose into the button controlling the paralysis cathode.

Zorba passed out.

I looked at him to see where I'd stabbed him. Both blades stuck clean through his knee, visible on both sides. Any other time I would've gotten queasy at the sight.

Retribution settled my stomach though.

"Come to me." TL sounded as though he'd adjusted to the pain of being stretched.

"You have three minutes," Wirenut informed us, "before he wakes back up."

I pushed to my knees. "How do you know?"

"I watched the clock when you knocked him out the first time.

The cathode's only good for two shots. Then the fuse has to be switched out. So when he wakes up, he wakes up."

Glancing at the wall-mounted clock, I made a mental note of the time and shuffled toward TL.

He wiggled his fingers. "Put your tool belt next to my right hand."

Lying down next to his hand, I scooted my thigh as close as I could.

"What do I need?" TL asked Wirenut.

"Get the number three giclo wrench," he answered. "Should be right in front."

TL's fingers slipped past one tool to the next, and he tugged it from its slot. "Got it."

There was no way I could identify a tool by touch. Hammer, sure. But a number three whatever wrench? No way.

He positioned the wrench between his thumb and forefinger. "Put your wrists next to my hand."

I checked the clock as I sat up. "One minute, fifty-eight seconds." I positioned my steel bands next to his fingers.

TL inserted the tool. "Wirenut?"

"Right ninety degrees. Left forty-five."

Two tiny *tings* and my hands were free. I grabbed the wrench from TL. "Same for my feet?"

Wirenut nodded. "Yes."

I took a couple of steady breaths and then slipped the tool into my feet bonds.

Right ninety degrees. Left forty-five. Two tiny *tings*, and I was free.

I jumped to my feet and glanced at the clock. One minute, one second.

"Wirenut first," TL instructed.

"Different locks. You need a four-point-one tes wrench."

"Four-point-one tes wrench? What the hell's a four-point-one tes wrench?" I reached down and yanked the belt off my thigh. I ran to Wirenut. "Show me."

Quickly, he scanned the tools. "Third from the left."

Pulling it out, I dropped the belt. "What do I do?"

"My right foot first. Insert the wrench into the foot bond one centimeter, click it left thirty degrees."

"One centimeter? Thirty degrees? Are you serious?" *I can't do this.*

"GiGi," TL barked. "Focus."

Oddly enough, his harsh tone didn't intimidate me. It zapped me full of confidence.

Ignoring the ticking time, I squatted at Wirenut's right foot. I inserted the wrench and clicked it left. *Ting.*

"Now my left foot. This time click it right, though."

I did.

Ting.

"Right wrist, clicking left again."

Ting.

I moved to his left hand. "Click it right. I got the pattern."

Ting.

As his iron bonds fell free, Wirenut dropped from the wall, and Zorba shot straight up.

Wirenut shoved me out of the way. "Get TL. Same pattern. I got Zorba."

I scrambled across the cement to TL. In my peripheral vision, Zorba jerked the sword from his knee right as Wirenut leapt.

My heart banging, I zeroed in on TL's restraints.

Right foot. Insert one centimeter. Click left thirty degrees. *Ting.*

Out of the corner of my eye, Wirenut kicked Zorba's hand. The sword sailed across the room and landed, handle down, in one of the candle urns.

I focused on TL's left foot. Clicked right. *Ting.*

Zorba punched Wirenut, snapping his head to the left.

I scooted over TL's body to his right hand, inserted the wrench, clicked left. *Ting.*

Wirenut whipped around and delivered a flying roundhouse to Zorba's stomach.

Left hand. Clicked right. *Ting.*

Zorba stumbled back a few feet and then came roaring forward, striking Wirenut's sternum and jaw at the same time.

TL's bonds fell away.

Grabbing his chest, Wirenut sucked in a breath, and Zorba sneered.

TL sprung to his feet, and Wirenut held up his hand. "Don't. He's mine."

Wirenut dropped to his knees, spun, and swept Zorba off his feet. The older man landed hard on the floor, his head thudding against the cement. Wirenut scrambled on top of him and rammed his elbow into Zorba's throat.

Gagging, Zorba reached up, seized Wirenut's hair, and yanked.

Gritting his jaw, Wirenut grabbed Zorba's head and slammed it into the cement again.

Sounds of bones crunching echoed through the chamber.

With my heart stampeding in my chest, I glanced over at TL. *Aren't we going to do something?*

He shook his head.

Zorba twisted his body and threw Wirenut off. He rolled across the floor.

Zorba staggered to his feet at the same time Wirenut jumped to his.

He rushed Zorba, pushing him across the room, right toward the sword and the urn. Wirenut shoved, and Zorba flew backward, straight onto the double-bladed, lion-engraved sword.

Both blades sliced clean through his back and straight out his stomach.

His body twitched and then slumped lifeless over the urn.

I turned away from the gory scene and covered my face with my hands.

Zorba's tool for sick, twisted pleasure had brought him to his end.

▦ ▦ ▦

TWENTY MINUTES LATER. Nalani cut through calm water, motoring us away from the private island back toward mainland Rissala.

Dark red lit the horizon where the sun would rise in the next thirty minutes or so. A thin layer of fog hovered on the water's surface. Under other circumstances, this would've been a beautiful, peaceful morning.

TL stood on the other side of the boat, talking on his cell phone. Wirenut sat beside me, arms folded, staring at the boat's floorboards.

He hadn't said one single word since exiting the mansion. I knew if I asked him if he was okay, he'd just nod his head. So I kept quiet and left him to his thoughts. He'd talk when he felt ready.

TL clicked off his cell phone. "Clean-up crew's on their way."

I furrowed my brow. "Clean-up crew?"

"They'll take care of the mansion, evidence, Zorba's body." TL connected the satellite and punched in the scrambler code.

Balancing the laptop in his lap, he took a seat between Wirenut and me. Chapling, David, and Beaker appeared on the screen. All three sets of eyes widened in matching shock.

In that second, I realized what we must look like. Wirenut shirtless, tiny nicks on his chest, bruised eye, scar on display. TL with a makeshift ear bandage, soaked through with blood.

And me with dried blood on my face and mouth, sporting a (I moved my tongue around) yep, missing tooth. I touched my forehead, grimacing at the knot.

"Um." Chapling cleared his throat. "Need I ask what happened?"

David frowned as he studied me, but didn't say anything.

I sent him a small smile to let him know I was okay. His frown softened to a slight curve of the lips.

TL punched a few keys. "I'm sending you a digital image of the sword. We have it here on board if you need a live shot."

"Okay, give me a sec." Chomping her gum, Beaker did some key strokes on her end. She zoomed in on the image TL had sent. "Code is in the handle. Million to one says it's engraved. That's thirty-three-hundred-strength sterling. Mix one part citeca acid to two parts riumba enzyme. Heat to one fifty Celsius. Coat handle with mixture using a rubber rod. It'll take three seconds, and you'll see the final message."

TL nodded. "Fantastic work, Beaker. Anything else?"

They all shook their heads.

"Signing off." TL closed the laptop and dialed his cell phone. He began a conversation in Rissalan.

I heard citeca acid and riumba enzyme. He was probably arranging to have those chemicals waiting when we got to our destination.

Nalani stuck her head out of the pilothouse. "Six minutes to dock." She tossed a duffel bag at us. "Clean up. You guys definitely need it."

I unzipped the duffel. Three sets of clean clothes lined the top; first-aid supplies scattered the bottom. I handed the guys their stuff and then stepped inside the pilothouse to change.

Nalani glanced at my thigh as I peeled my wet suit down. "You'll need a couple stitches and some antibiotics. Tape it together for now. Bandage it up good. Let me see your mouth."

I opened wide.

She whistled. "Tore the root out and everything. It's a molar. Don't worry about it. We'll get you a replacement."

I wiped my face with a wet nap. "What about TL?" That slice had been bloody.

Nalani idled down. "You'd be surprised what plastic surgeons can do. Everyone'll be good as new in no time. Hurry and put on your clothes. We're almost there."

Over my bathing suit I slipped on an island dress. Similar to the flowy, gauzy ones the locals wore.

Nalani pulled the boat alongside a rocky slope.

Wirenut and I followed TL over the rocks, up to a dirt road where a car waited. Behind us Nalani motored off in the opposite direction. She'd done the same thing in Ushbania. Just disappeared.

This time I knew I'd see her again.

We climbed into the car, TL cranked the engine, and we were off. He cut across a field and into the woods. Twenty minutes later we parked behind a stone shack hidden in thick overgrowth.

"Safe house. Katarina's here. She turned herself in. We had a local agent bring her here." TL opened his door. "Let's go."

We helped TL cover the car with bushy tree branches and then followed him inside.

Katarina sat in the corner of the shadowed shack, handcuffed to a pipe coming from the floor. Still dressed in her black burglar suit, she glanced up and quickly looked away.

What an awful girl.

A short man handed TL a canvas bag, said something in Rissalan, and exited through a hidden panel in the floor.

TL unwrapped the sword and laid it on the only table in the shack. He emptied the canvas bag, too. Chemicals, burners, stir sticks, and tubes fell out. All the things Beaker had said we'd need.

I sat on the floor and cranked up the laptop, ready to decipher the last encrypted message.

Wirenut and TL worked in silence. Mixing chemicals, heating them. Wirenut stuck a thermometer in the liquid, and they waited, watching the temperature.

"One fifty." He nodded.

TL spread the smoking mixture on the sword's handle. Three seconds ticked by. I placed my fingers on the laptop's keys.

He held a magnifying glass to the handle. "Five one two. Three spaces. One zero one two. Two spaces. One five one two. One space. Two zero . . ."

TL continued reading off the number patterns, and I typed. One hundred sequences in all. A lot of data crammed onto the handle of a sword.

I went to work. My fingers raced over the keypad. I wove in and out of security barriers, tunneled through safeguards, zoomed around blocked systems. I designated principles, specified components, wrapped codexes. I stranded screeds, followed copeperis, formatted algorithms.

"Got it." *Clickclickclick.* "The neurotoxin is on the other side of the world. It's located on a sailboat in the Pacific five miles from Myralap Island."

"Great job, GiGi." TL dialed his phone and gave the information to the government's retrieval team he'd hired.

I put down my laptop and stood, stretching my fatigued muscles. Another successful mission gone by.

Clicking his phone off, TL turned to Katarina. "Who are you?"

She didn't look up. "Katarina Leosi."

"Why did you turn yourself in? Why did you disengage the mansion's explosives?"

Katarina's shoulders slumped. Her patheticness didn't faze me.

"I thought my father was collecting rare art pieces. I didn't know about Stan or the stolen neurotoxin or Papa's deceit."

TL put his phone on the table. "Who, exactly, did you think your father was?"

"A businessman. An art collector. A descendant of a long line of famous burglars. He was training me to follow in his footsteps."

"And you're okay with being trained into a life of crime?"

She closed her eyes. "It was his dying wish. I lost my real parents when I was a baby. He took me in. He's the only father I've ever known."

"He wasn't dying. He lied to you."

Long pause. "I know that now," she murmured.

I glanced across the shack at Wirenut. He stood with his back to us, staring out the dirty window. He and Katarina weren't cousins after all. Interesting.

So Zorba killed Wirenut's family, moved to Rissala, and took in a baby girl? It didn't make sense.

I stepped forward. "Can I ask a question?"

TL nodded.

"Why did Zorba raise you?"

Katarina finally looked up. Sorrow and bewilderment weighed heavy in her eyes. It softened my heart a little.

"He told me my real father worked for him. He said he was responsible for my parents' deaths." She lifted a shoulder. "That's all I know."

TL stepped up next to me. "Who did you think Stan was?"

"Who he said he was, a guy here on vacation."

"And the Ghost?"

"Another burglar after the same pieces we were. I copycatted him, trying to keep the trail off me. I had no idea Stan and the Ghost were one and the same."

TL crossed his arms over his chest. "And you considered poisoning him fair play?"

"No! Of course not." She looked over at Wirenut. "I'm so sorry. I never meant to hurt you."

He turned from the window. An unreadable expression blanked his face. "Then why poison me?"

Katarina quietly sighed. "Papa told me the Ghost was selling the artifacts and funding terrorism."

"What about the last time I saw you? You said your father saw us in the marketplace? Zorba was there?"

"He was. I had no idea. He saw us talking and got really mad. I've never seen him so angry. It scared me. But . . . what was I supposed to tell you? That I was a burglar?" Her voice cracked. "That I really like you?" She ducked her head, sniffed.

Wirenut didn't say anything in response, just stood staring at her.

"And the messages?" I asked. "Didn't you wonder about the paper hidden in the egg and the jewel?"

"When I found the paper in the egg, I asked Papa about it. He said the paper meant nothing to the Ghost without the artifact. And then before I went in to get the crown, Papa told me there was a replica of the ruby from the crown I needed to leave behind. I didn't ask any questions; I figured he knew what he was talking about."

Seemed to me Katarina was a manipulated pawn like the rest of us. Only more so. She'd been lied to her whole life.

That is, if she's actually telling the truth now.

The shack's door opened. An old, gray-haired woman appeared. Something about her seemed familiar. I studied her as she closed the door and crossed the short distance to where we stood.

TL acknowledged her with a nod.

"You're the jewelry lady from the market," I realized aloud. *How funny.* I'd had no idea.

She winked at me and then leveled Katarina with a hard glare. "I'm Special Agent Pierson. You're in my care now. *Don't* underestimate me based on my age."

I was glad that lethal glare wasn't aimed in my direction.

"Let's go." TL grabbed his cell phone and headed from the stone shack.

Wirenut and I followed. He didn't take a last look at Katarina, but I did. She still sat with her head dropped, shoulders slumped.

I felt sorry for her. How lost she must feel.

After I helped the guys uncover the car, we climbed in and drove off.

I rolled down my window. Cool morning air flowed in. "What's going to happen to Katarina?"

TL shifted gears. "If her story checks out, she'll go free."

"Free where? She doesn't have any family."

TL turned onto the coastal highway. "She'll become part of the system."

Part of the system? That sucked. Not a lifestyle I'd wish on anybody. "And if her story doesn't check out?"

"She'll be tried as an adult. Depending on what she's involved in of Zorba's, she could face the death penalty."

I blinked. *The death penalty? Whoa.*

In the backseat, Wirenut lay down. He put his arm over his

eyes and turned his head away. The sunlight brought out his facial bruises, where Zorba had punched him.

I wanted so badly for Wirenut to be okay. I wanted to see him smile, hear his smart-aleck remarks, watch him do his victory shoulder-roll dance.

"We got in a car accident," TL informed us, "in case anyone asks."

The next morning, we caught a flight back to America and unfortunately got grounded in Chicago because of bad weather. We got a hotel for the night and grabbed a plane to California early the next day. As we were pulling up to the ranch's iron gate, I breathed a sigh of relief.

Home.

TL slipped a remote from his jacket pocket and punched in his personal code. The gate slowly swept open, and we pulled through.

It swung closed behind us as we made our way up the long driveway.

Off to the left Bruiser bounced along on a riding mower, doing her afternoon chores. The machine dwarfed her tiny body, making her look like a little girl. She caught sight of us and enthusiastically waved. I waved back.

Hard to believe we'd been gone only about a week. Seemed like a month at least.

Beyond her in the corral, Parrot washed one of the thoroughbreds. Funny that a guy with horrible hay allergies loved horses so much.

Beside the corral the barn sat wide open. Jonathan was inside, punching a hanging bag. I checked my watch. 4:00 P.M. It'd be time for PT in another thirty minutes. Wonder what kind of muscle-screaming torture he had in mind for everyone today?

I squinted but didn't see David. He usually warmed up with Jonathan before PT.

TL circled around the driveway and parked in front of the sprawling, one-story ranch house.

Mystic came around the side, garden tools in hand. He'd been tending his herb garden.

I smiled, realizing I'd missed everyone.

Beaker stepped out the front door, chomping gum, sporting a black-and-white-striped Mohawk.

Okay, I'd missed *almost* everyone.

TL opened the driver's door and got out.

Wirenut leaned up from the backseat. He put his hand on my shoulder. "Don't tell anybody about what happened. About me, Zorba, Katarina. Anything. I don't want anybody to know."

I nodded. "You don't have to worry about that with me."

I didn't bother reminding him that we weren't *allowed* to speak of the details.

We climbed from the car as TL popped the trunk. "You two are excused from PT. Get some rest." He handed us each our oversized backpacks.

Wirenut shouldered his. "I'll be in my room." He brushed past Beaker with barely a hello.

She frowned. "What's up with him?"

Where's my knuckle rub? I knew she was thinking. Wirenut always knuckle-rubbed Beaker's head. And she loved it, even though she pretended not to.

"He's tired. That's all." I zipped up my windbreaker.

"I'd still say hi to him," Beaker grumbled, shuffling off, "even if *I* were tired."

Carting my pack through the door, I surreptitiously glanced around. I didn't want David to catch me looking for him. I wanted to "accidentally" run into him.

I peeked into the dining hall, a miniature version of a school cafeteria. Its aluminum table and chairs sat empty. Two hours from now the place would come alive with people eating, talking, laughing.

I slipped across the hall into the common area. Empty, too. No one watching TV, shooting pool, or playing cards. Later this evening Parrot and Bruiser would definitely be here, continuing their ongoing air-hockey match.

I passed by the mountainous mural that hid our elevator to the below-ground levels. Maybe David was down there with Chapling.

Okay, game plan: drop my things in the girls' room and then go to the computer lab where I'd "accidentally" run into David.

Rolling my eyes, I strode down the hall to the girls' room. David's room sat two doors down on the left. From my vantage point the door stood open. What could be my reason for *having* to go down there?

I lingered, studying his open door, coming up blank. There

really was no reason for me to go down there. What would be my excuse?

Except to say hi, of course.

But I wanted *him* to find *me*. Not the other way around.

Stupid. *I know.*

And childish.

But . . . here went nothing.

I coughed.

He didn't come out.

I sneezed.

Nothing.

I cleared my throat.

Nada.

"GiGi?"

I jerked around. *David.* My stomach leap-frogged to my throat. If it weren't for my lips being closed, it probably would have boinged right out of my mouth.

I swallowed. "Hi."

Okay, that came across good. Calm. Casual. Not too excited. Not too nervous. It sounded I-missed-you-but-not-desperately. The tone was definitely I'm-my-own-woman.

Mentally, I gave myself one firm, agreeable nod.

His lips were moving. *Crap.* He was talking, and I missed it.

David's lips stopped moving.

He waited.

He wanted me to respond. *Double crap.*

I cleared my throat. "Sorry, what'd you say?"

David quirked a smile. "I said, what are you doing?"

"Um . . ." I shrugged. "Getting home just." I shook my head. "I mean, just getting home."

Inwardly, I sighed. *Guess I'm not my own woman.*

His dark eyes dropped to my lips. "Heard you're missing a tooth."

I gave a jerky nod.

He took a step toward me, staring at my lips, and my heart revved to light speed. *Please let my lips look good right now.*

"Can I see?"

I blinked. "What . . . no!" *Gross.*

He laughed. "Are you relaxed now?"

I laughed, too. I couldn't help it. He knew me too well.

Taking my pack, he gave me a quick hug and a kiss on my head. "Missed you."

His cologne swirled into my senses, and I wanted to hold on longer. "I missed you, too."

David had no *idea* how much I'd missed him. It'd probably scare him if he knew. Like, my-girlfriend's-freakishly-obsessed-with-me kind of scare.

Then again I wasn't his girlfriend. Not officially.

Yet.

He led the way into the girls' room. "Did you get my little surprise?"

The hidden lollipop. Thinking of you. "Yes." I smiled. "Thank you so much. That was very sweet."

David put my stuff on the floor. "So did you?"

"Did I what?"

He sat down on my bed. "Think of me?"

Only every second of every moment of every day. "Yes."

"A lot?"

I laughed. "Yes. *Sheesh,* what do you want from me? Yes, I thought of you. A lot. Happy?"

"I'm getting there."

I'm getting there. What did that mean?

I put my hands on my hips. "Did you think of me?" *I can't believe I asked him that question.*

It felt good. Bold. Sexy of me.

"Yeah." He held out his hand. "Come 'ere."

My stomach cycloned as I crossed the room and took his hand.

He tugged me down beside him, reached under my bed, and brought out—

A lollipop bouquet! Full of dozens of suckers. Raspberry, cherry, watermelon, lemon, mango, passion fruit, apple, banana, and I don't know how many more.

"For you." He put it in my lap.

"I can't believe you did this." I threw my arms around his neck. "Thank you."

He squeezed me tight. "You're very welcome."

Someone rapped on the open door, and we pulled apart.

Bruiser grinned. "I see you got your surprise."

David shot her a playful glare. "Your roommate's a real pest. She's been in my face all week long, like an annoying gnat."

Bruiser batted her lashes. "I'm really glad you're back. Coming to PT?"

"Definitely." I put my lollipops on my nightstand. "Let me change."

David stood. "You don't have to."

"I know. Never thought I'd actually say this, but I *want* to."

Bruiser and David gave me matching are-you-kidding-me looks.

I laughed. "Really. I *do*."

Suddenly, David's cell buzzed. At the same time, so did mine. We checked the displays.

TL's stat code.

13

David and I rushed off the elevator and to the conference room. We opened the door just as TL came out.

"Have a seat. Chapling and I will be right in."

David and I sat on the right side of the table. Neither of us mumbled a sound as we waited.

What's going on? Another mission? Already?

It couldn't be. We hadn't even been home a couple of hours yet.

Wirenut appeared in the door. "Got the page. What's up?"

We shrugged.

Wirenut took a seat across from us.

A couple of weeks ago David, Wirenut, and I had been in this conference room finding out about the neurotoxin for the very first time. Wirenut had been fidgety, restless, nervous. Looking at him now you'd never guess he had been any other way but calm and collected.

TL entered the conference room with Chapling hobbling behind him.

He climbed up into the chair beside me and leaned in. "Welcome home," he whispered.

Thanks, I mouthed back. Gosh, I'd missed his little, frizzy-headed self.

TL pressed a button on the remote-control panel housed within the table. The back wall slid open, revealing a wide flat screen.

Katarina appeared.

I glanced at Wirenut. His brow twitched. Other than that he showed no emotion.

"Specialists," TL began, "Katarina Leosi has been found innocent of all charges related to Antonio Badaduchi, aka Octavias Zorba."

I sent her a small smile to let her know I was glad for her. Way down deep inside I knew she was a good guy. And I'd been right.

"Katarina," TL continued, "has found three documents in her bedroom that have prompted her to contact us." TL nodded to the screen. "Go ahead."

She cleared her throat. "Approximately forty-five minutes ago while packing my belongings, I found documents hidden in a secret compartment of my dresser. I wasn't aware my fath— Octavias knew I had a secret compartment. Perhaps he hid these papers there because he knew his office contents would be confiscated if anything went wrong."

Katarina's image slid to the screen's upper-left corner. Three images of handwritten paper appeared in the center of the screen. "This is Octavias's writing. I'm sure he handwrote them to avoid a computer trail. They're in code. From my limited knowledge of cryptography, I pieced together they're about Stan, or Frankie as I now know is his real name. That's when I contacted you."

"Thank you, Katarina," TL said.

With a slight nod, she disappeared from the screen.

Chapling raised a finger. "That's where I come in. I've deciphered only page one. What I found, though, stopped me in my tracks."

TL propped his fingers on the table. "Zorba admitted he devised the neurotoxin plan in order to flush out Wirenut. What has had us perplexed and Chapling working extra hard is how Zorba initially located Wirenut. How Zorba knew Wirenut was here in San Belden, California."

Chapling pushed away from the table. He waddled over to the screen. From his pocket he slipped a metal retractor and expanded it.

He touched document one, enlarging it to full screen. Then he tapped it again, zooming in on one single line. "This is line five."

Again with the number five. Quickly, I read the code, isolating the prime numbers, matching them to letters of the alphabet. I yanked my notepad and pencil from my sweatshirt pocket, scribbled the letters. And sucked in a breath.

Everyone looked at me.

Chapling retracted his pointer. "GiGi, tell your team what you just figured out."

No. It couldn't be. I glanced at TL for confirmation, and he nodded his go ahead.

"Th-there's an insider." *Oh. My. God.*

Wirenut straightened in his chair. "An insider? What are you talking about?"

TL leaned forward. "Someone on this ranch leaked information that the Ghost is here in San Belden. When Zorba heard, he composed his twisted charade."

Wirenut shot to his feet. "Who?"

"We don't know." TL's face hardened. "Yet."

"But why? Why would someone do that to me?"

"I seriously doubt this was personal. Whoever released your whereabouts did it for money." TL's phone beeped. He checked the LCD. "I think you forget how famous the Ghost was. *Is* still. People, the media, would pay big money to know who you are. My only hope is that your true identity hasn't been leaked as well."

Minutes later, Chapling and I stood in front of the wide screen studying pages two and three of the handwritten documents. Strange letters and numbers I'd never seen before. Not English, nor Rissalan.

"What other language would Zorba write in?"

Chapling sniffed. "He was an international terrorist. There's no telling how many languages he knew."

"Why would he compose document one in English and the other two in a different language?" I scrunched my brow. "Doesn't make sense. Unless they're in different languages because they're about different things. Could Parrot help translate these?"

"Why, when we have our computer," Chapling said, smiling. In the screen's upper-right corner, the computer continued scrolling through international records, searching for an identifiable language.

"My guess is that Zorba *wanted* us to easily decipher page one. He wanted us to know he had an insider." Chapling took out a tissue and blew his nose. "Zorba liked games. He planned on pages two and three being a puzzle. My gut says that whatever's encrypted there is very important. Life or death."

"Got it." I spun around. "Wiren—"

The conference room sat empty. I'd forgotten everybody had left Chapling and me to our work.

I took my phone and punched a series of buttons. "I'm texting Wirenut to get down here."

We continued scrutinizing the documents while we waited on Wirenut.

I looked down at Chapling. "You got a cold?"

He rubbed his nose. "Little one."

"Taking medication?"

"Over the counter."

"Laying off the caffeine? Getting rest?" Chapling was twice my age. *Look who's taking care of whom?*

"What's going on?" Wirenut stepped into the room.

I waved him over. "Come look at these."

He approached and Chapling quickly explained the situation while Wirenut examined the documents.

"The language is vaguely familiar." Wirenut moved a step

closer and perused the screen. "I'll be right back." He raced from the room.

In the upper-right-hand corner, the computer continued scrolling. Whatever Zorba had used was buried deep. Could be some old-world dialect of an ancient culture. "Wonder how many different languages and dialects there are in the world?"

Chapling sneezed. "Including biblical times? Thousands. Easily."

Wow.

Wirenut zipped back into the room and over to the screen. He held up a small silver bracelet next to the documents. "I wore this home from the hospital when I was a baby. It's from my mom."

I squinted. Tiny letters engraved the back of the nameplate. "What's it say?"

"It's a prayer. *'Lex fic nisabs dosoqua.'* May God protect your future."

Chapling pulled a tissue wad from his pocket. "Looks a lot older than you."

"It is. It's been passed down from generation to generation. Every time a boy is born it passes on."

I shifted closer to get a better look. "You're the youngest of five boys. All of them wore this, too?"

Wirenut nodded.

A chill shivered my body. *May God protect your future.* Ironic that Wirenut was the last to receive it and the only survivor of his uncle's wrath.

Wirenut rotated it, catching the light. "Someday my son will wear it, too."

His sentiment brought a smile to my face. "What's the language?"

"Kusem. I don't think it's spoken anymore."

I extended my hand. "May I?"

With a nod, Wirenut gave it to me.

Holding the lightweight bracelet to the screen, I compared the letters and symbols. "It's a match."

"Oh good. Goodgoodgoodgoodgood." From his shirt pocket, Chapling slipped a silver mike resembling a mechanical pencil. "Daisy," he spoke into the eraser end. "Halt."

The computer stopped scrolling.

Daisy? I mouthed.

"*Dukes of Hazzard*. It's the only show I watched as a kid." He shrugged sheepishly. "Always had a thing for the female Duke cousin."

Wirenut and I exchanged amused glances. I had no idea Chapling had named our ranch computer.

"Do the other guys call it Daisy, too?"

Chapling waggled his brows. "What guy doesn't have a thing for Daisy Duke?"

"Well, I don't want to be the odd one out." I took the microphone. "Hello, Daisy. Sorry I didn't know your name before."

THAT'S OKAY, the computer typed. HOW CAN I HELP YOU?

"Search language Kusem. K-u-s-e-m." I glanced at Wirenut for spelling confirmation, and he nodded.

Daisy scrolled. KUSEM LOCATED.

"Good work. Translate documents two and three. Print to computer lab."

Daisy's screen strobed. PRINTING NOW.

Chapling rapid-fire clapped. "Oh, she's fast. Fastfastfast."

I handed him the mike. "Imagine the world before computers."

He shrieked, "Perish the thought."

I laughed. "Let me change and I'll meet you in the lab." I needed to get out of the clothes I'd worn home from Chicago.

We crossed the conference room to the door. At the elevator, Chapling went back to the lab and I punched in my personal code, placed my hand on the fingerprint-identification panel, and rode it up four floors with Wirenut. We stepped off and halted in our tracks.

In total silence, every member of Specialist Teams One and Two lined the hallway. No one had changed from their PT clothes.

David stood at the very end near his room. He caught sight of Wirenut and me and came down the hall toward us.

"What's going on?" I whispered.

"Lock down. TL's searching our belongings."

What? "You mean . . . like everything?" *Underwear, bras, tampons?*

"Yep, everything."

I closed my eyes on a silent groan. I had *so* many dirty clothes. "Even your stuff?"

David lifted his brows. "Can't trust anyone when there's been a breach in security."

Yeah. But David? He's TL's right-hand guy. "You're okay with that? Not being trusted?"

"GiGi, it's part of this life. Even Jonathan and Chapling get searched, and they have the same clearance level as TL."

"What about TL? Him, too?"

"Yes. Someone higher up will search him. This is serious business. And it won't stop here. The barn, the house, the property, the rooms below us. The entire place will be thoroughly investigated."

Wow.

TL stepped from one of the guy's room. He looked down the hall right at me. "What are you both doing up here?"

All eyes turned to me.

I swallowed. "I-I change clothes wanted to." I shook my head. "I mean, I wanted to change clothes." Seemed like a good idea at the time.

"You and Chapling are supposed to be working on the documents. You were given a job." TL crossed the hall and unlocked the door to the room I shared with Bruiser and Beaker. "Get to it, and Wirenut get in line."

"Yes, sir," we both mumbled, completely humiliated.

As Wirenut shuffled over to get in line, David turned his back to everyone, blocking me from their view. He linked pinkies with me and gave my little finger a quick squeeze. Somehow that gesture made me want to smile and cry at the same time.

"Don't take it personally," he whispered. "TL's extremely irritated right now."

I nodded. But all I really wanted to do was bury my head in code for like a million years. Or maybe bury my head in David's chest for the same amount of time.

Minutes later, I shuffled into the lab Chapling and I used. He sat hunched over his workstation, his fingers racing across the keyboard. I imagined that's what I looked like when I existed in my zone.

Except for the whole he's-a-red-headed-little-person-and-I'm-not thing.

I rolled my chair out. "Hey."

He jerked straight up. "Ow!" And grabbed his neck. "Whiplash."

Jeez, you'd think I'd screamed the greeting.

"Genius at work here. Heeelllooo? Give a warning next time." He scratched his head, making his Brillo-pad hair poof out.

"You need a haircut."

He waved me off. "Yeahyeahyeah." He tapped his screen. "I'm working on the documents. You get cranking with phone records, postal, e-mail. Any communication between San Belden, California, and Rissala. We got an insider to nail."

I slipped on my glasses and dove into cyberspace.

I visited the San Belden Phone Company first. Tried a couple of commonly used passwords to enter their system. Broke through on the fourth try.

Their IT guys needed a lesson in password protection.

Zipping through the past twelve months of phone calls, I isolated the ones to and from Rissala, tracing each one. Standard stuff. Family, friends, a few business calls.

I skimmed the numbers and matched them to the Rissalan police department, newspaper, radio, and TV. I hacked into police records . . . and silently laughed. Reporters from all over the world were bugging them for news on the break-ins and the Ghost.

Leaving the police records, I wove my way in and out of ISP servers. Lots and lots of e-mails to and from Rissala. Again, standard stuff. Family communication. Friends. And, of course, reporters looking for breaking news.

"Wait. What's this? A pellucid image?"

I clicked a couple keys. Someone sent an alias e-mail and then wiped the image from the server. *Idiot*. Didn't they know that nothing was ever truly wiped clean?

My heart revved as my fingers clicked away. *I'm onto something. I'm* definitely *onto something.* The e-mail was sent from a coffeehouse in town.

Sequestering the message, I ran it through a clarity program. At the same time I brought up the coffeehouse security cameras and scrolled the archives until I located the time matching the e-mail's time/date stamp.

The clarity program dinged. I scanned the message. Definitely about the Ghost. I selected the camera archive link. A picture popped up on my screen.

I sucked in a breath. *Oh no.*

"The documents." Chapling looked up from his screen, his eyes wide with numb shock. "We've got to get TL. Now."

"I'm right here."

Chapling and I jerked around. TL stood inside the door. How long had he been there? I hadn't even heard him come in. I glanced at my watch. Hours had gone by.

He came toward me, staring at my screen. "Is that the insider?"

"Yes, sir."

With a hard jaw, TL turned to Chapling. "And the documents?"

"There's neurotoxin. Here on the ranch. Set to be released at thirteen hundred hours tomorrow. According to the document, Katarina and Wirenut have to be together when it's found."

14

MINUTES LATER, WE STOOD in the conference room waiting in silence.

The door opened, and David escorted Erin in. Jonathan took her and pushed her down into the chair at the head of the table.

Along the back wall I stood beside Wirenut, silently observing. Immediately, I recalled my arrest months ago before the Specialists had recruited me. How roughly the cops had treated me. How frightened I'd been. Erin must be petrified right now. The only difference was that she deserved it.

Disgust and anger rolled through me at that thought. How could she have done it? *Why* would she have done it? No amount of money, *no* amount, was worth it. We were family. Didn't she care? I would never, *never*, intentionally harm anyone at this ranch.

TL took the seat to her right. "You *know* why you're here. Don't even *think* about playing games with me." He leveled lethal eyes on her. "What is your connection with Octavias Zorba?"

Silence. Erin didn't blink. Twitch. Speak. Nothing.

A minute passed as she kept her expressionless gaze on TL.

He switched his focus beyond her shoulder to Jonathan and gave a barely discernible nod.

Jonathan placed his finger on the back of her neck, and she screamed.

Every muscle in my body contracted at the painful wail. She's a traitor, I reminded myself, concentrating on keeping my face reactionless.

He stepped away, and Erin slumped forward.

"Sit up," TL snapped.

Pulling her shoulders back, she tossed her dark hair, like she'd just finished blowing it dry or something. A smirk replaced her expressionless face.

I watched her, unable to wrap my brain completely around her new facade. This was an Erin I'd never seen. She seemed . . . demented.

TL propped his hands on the table, appearing unfazed by her dramatics. "What is your connection with Octavias Zorba?"

Silence. Again. Other than her smirk, she made no response.

TL shot from his chair, grabbed her hair, and pulled her head back.

I caught my breath. I'd never seen him get violent with one of us. If Erin's momentary shock held any indication, neither had she.

He stuck his hard face an inch from hers. "Zorba's dead. You're not going to get whatever it is he promised you."

She sneered. "How do you know I haven't already got it?"

"You're a fool to admit it if you did. You're an even bigger fool if you think I believe it. Zorba wasn't stupid. He wouldn't pay up until a job was done." TL leaned a fraction closer. "What you don't seem to comprehend is that his *pay up* wouldn't be what you're expecting. He'd think nothing of slicing his sword through your pretty little body."

I cringed at the mention of the sword. More than anything I wanted to turn to Wirenut and make sure he was okay. But I kept myself still, wishing any gory flashbacks from his brain.

Erin swallowed, and TL tracked the movement with his eyes. "Scared? Good. What'd you think? You wouldn't get caught? Zorba'd rescue you? You wouldn't go to prison? You wouldn't die?"

"You can't harm me," she snipped.

With a humorless chuckle, TL released her and stepped back. "Erin, you're not new to this. You know my powers. I can make you disappear. Forever."

She glanced over her shoulder at David. I couldn't see her face, but he held her glance with a flat stare. It was all part of a facade, knowing how to put your emotions aside in a tense situation. TL was the master of it. I knew David's expressions, though, and saw the hurt and confusion deep in his eyes.

What was he thinking? I mean, here sat one of his teammates, a former girlfriend at that. A girl he'd trained with and lived with for years, and she'd crossed to the other side.

It'd be like Wirenut or Parrot, Bruiser, Mystic, or even Beaker going bad. I'd be crushed. Betrayed. Confused. And I'd known them for only a few months. David and Erin had known each other a lot longer.

TL folded his arms across his chest. "We know you sent an anonymous e-mail to the press about the Ghost. We know hundreds of reporters contacted you offering money for Wirenut's true identity. We know you started a bidding war. We know Zorba heard of this and devised his plan to flush out Wirenut. We know Zorba contacted you while we were over in Rissala. We know he offered you two million dollars to hide the neurotoxin on the ranch."

TL cocked his head. "Would you like to know how we know all this?"

Erin lifted her brows.

"Because you're STUPID!"

Everyone but Jonathan jerked at TL's sudden temper. I'd *never* heard him yell like this.

He clamped his hand around her neck. "Every one of your e-mails left a pellucid image. GiGi found them all." He got right in Erin's face. "You disgust me. I can't believe I even *considered* you for the Specialists."

I would die if TL ever said something like that to me.

He squeezed her neck. "Where's the toxin?"

She shook her head.

TL applied more pressure. "Where's the toxin?"

Erin gasped.

He squeezed harder. "Where's the toxin?"

Red splotches crept up her cheeks and across her forehead.

Still standing along the back wall, I concentrated on keeping my body and face stoic. As if none of this fazed me. Inside, though, my heart raced, nearly deafening me with its uncontrollable banging.

How far would TL take things? And . . . did I really want to watch? It'd been different with Zorba and in Ushbania with Romanov Schalmosky. I really hadn't cared about their welfare. They were horrible, horrible men.

This, though? I *knew* Erin. Even if she *was* bad now. It'd be like Bruiser sitting there being strangled by TL. I'd find it extremely hard just to stand here and watch.

TL knows what he's doing, I reminded myself. *You have to trust his tactics. He* knows *Erin. He knows what will work. Thousands of lives are at stake.*

His bicep contracted. Veins popped on his hand and forearm. Erin's eyes glazed over with an eerie, unfocused gaze.

He's squeezing the life out of her.

I tried to swallow, but my throat had swelled with dryness. Dragging my eyes off TL and Erin, I focused behind them on David.

With a stiff jaw and clenched fists, he stared unblinking at a spot above my head. Clearly, this bothered him as much as me.

"Okay," she wheezed.

David's eyes snapped down to her and so did mine.

"I won't stop next time." TL eased the pressure. "What do you have to say?"

Erin gagged. "I . . . c-can't . . . breathe."

"I don't care." He retightened his grip. "What do you have to say?"

She gurgled. "To-xin . . . buried . . ."

After she choked out the coordinates, TL released her. "Get her out of my sight."

Erin grabbed her neck, wheezing for air.

Wrenching her out of the chair, Jonathan led her from the room.

What's going to happen to her? I wanted to ask, but I kept quiet, waiting for TL's instructions.

He checked his watch. "Let's go."

⠿ ⠿ ⠿

STANDING IN THE SOUTHWEST corner of the ranch's property, I stared at the coordinates Erin had given: 122.04.70 north, 38.18.70 west. A patch of moonlit grass.

TL flipped on a flashlight. "There's no evidence the dirt has been disturbed."

David tucked his hands in his jacket. "You think Erin lied? That nothing's buried here?"

"What about injection?" Wirenut squatted down. "A small toxin vial could be inserted, leaving the area virtually untouched."

"Let's X-ray." TL pressed the talk button on his two-way radio. "Chapling, cue satellite. You've got the coordinates. Let's see what's below us."

"Satellite cued," Chapling answered through the radio.

Opening my mini-laptop, I watched the dark screen. Seconds later a black-and-white picture flicked into view. "Upload complete."

The guys moved in around me to see. David, TL, Wirenut, and I appeared as phantom images. I had a weird urge to wave, just to see myself move.

Rows of piping and wiring tunneled the earth beneath us, everything the ranch needed for security.

"There it is." Wirenut pointed over my shoulder at the screen.

Slipping on my glasses, I leaned in. Sure enough, a tube of liquid lay about a foot beneath us. Scary to think that small amount could infect and kill everyone here at the ranch. As well as the city of San Belden and beyond.

"Huh." Wirenut tapped the screen. "See those two wires? One coming out the top of the vial and the other the bottom."

I nodded.

"Those are hematosis detectors."

Hematosis detectors?

"They're still under development. No one's actually used them yet."

"Um, not to be ignorant here, but what are hematosis detectors?" I seemed to be the only one who *didn't* know.

"Hematosis detectors," TL explained, "are a security measure, programmed to unlock with certain blood, certain DNA. They can be used on anything: explosives, government documents, safety deposit boxes."

I propped my glasses on top of my head. "According to Zorba's documents both Katarina and Wirenut have to be present to disarm the toxin. So obviously we're going to need both their blood." It all made sense now.

Wirenut moved away. "Couple of issues we're looking at here. Number one: hematosis detectors are *still under development*, meaning they've never been documented successful. Basically, we're doing a trial here. There's no proof they'll work. Number two: these detectors are rigged to read a certain number of drops."

"Five." The number popped into my head and out my mouth. Everyone looked at me.

"Zorba's theme has been five." I closed the laptop. "How much you wanna bet it's five here, too? Five drops of blood." *Oooh, I'm good.*

Wirenut smoothed his fingers down his goatee. "Okay, so going with that, there're two detectors. Each has to get the same number of drops. Five of me, five of Katarina."

Sounds easy enough.

He blew out a quick breath. "Only problem is—"

Why does there always have to be a problem?

"My blood and Katarina's have to hit the detectors in sync. Neither of us can be off by one tiny millisecond. The documents said thirteen hundred hours. That means the first drops have to touch at that exact second and then every five seconds, staying with the theme, after that."

"B-but what if something goes wrong? What if I'm not right about the number five? What if the vial's timer chip isn't calibrated to our clocks? What if your blood doesn't drop in sync? An-and you said this thing's still under development. What if it shorts out?" *Do they not see all this?*

TL flipped off the flashlight. "Then we all die."

⁂

HOUrs LATEr, KATArina's helicopter from the airport crossed over the ranch's border. Squinting against the whirling dust and grass, I held my hair back and checked my watch. 12:30 P.M.

Only thirty minutes until the toxin releases.

The helicopter touched down on a cleared area behind the house. The passenger door opened, and Katarina jumped down. Gripping her leather jacket together, she ran toward TL, David, Wirenut, and me.

"Hello," she yelled over the loud whipping.

I gave her a welcoming hug.

It surprised her, and for a second she didn't return the gesture. "Thank you," she mumbled, squeezing me quick.

Behind her, the copter lifted off.

"Hey." Wirenut smiled a little.

She smiled back. "Hey."

TL and Katarina exchanged handshakes, and he introduced David.

TL pointed to his truck. "Our protective gear is in the back. Get it on, and let's move out."

We all zipped into thick white suits with clear facial hoods and put on gloves. We hopped in the back of the truck and barreled over the ranch's property to the southwest corner. As we bounced along, Wirenut briefed Katarina on the hematosis detectors.

TL pulled to a stop, and we all piled out.

"Get your laptop, GiGi." TL pressed his two-way radio. "Chapling, give us our X-ray."

I opened my computer. The image flicked into view. "Got it."

TL handed Wirenut a garden shovel. "You're up."

Wirenut knelt at the patch of grass. He inserted the shovel a tiny bit and then quickly removed it. Rotating to the right, he inserted the shovel again and removed it. Quickly, he moved around and around the vial, keeping the same rhythm, each time the shovel going in a little farther.

On the laptop I watched his phantom image and the sharpness of the shovel as he got closer and closer to the vial. Almost a little *too* close.

What if he accidentally nicks it?

The dangerous thought jumped into my head, and I immediately shoved it right back out. He knows what he's doing, I reminded myself, although my pounding heart didn't quite believe my rationale. Accidents *did* happen, after all.

Wirenut inserted the shovel and left it there. "Let me see."

I knelt beside him, showing him the X-ray.

Sweat trickled down his forehead. "We're good."

I glanced at the laptop's digital time and caught my breath. "It's twelve fifty-one." I hadn't realized that so much time had gone by.

Wirenut nodded. "I know."

"B-but that's only nine minutes." *Nine minutes.* To remove all this dirt, patch into the time chip, drop the blood. And the time chip might be seconds or even minutes off. So we could really only have like five minutes to go. *Hello?*

Wirenut gripped my knee through the protective suit. "GiGi."

I jerked my focus from the shovel to his eyes.

"Listen to me and hear me good when I say this."

I swallowed.

"I lost one family. I *won't* lose another." He squeezed my knee. "Now let's get this done."

The conviction in his tone washed over me in a settling wave. *We're going to be okay.*

He took the shovel from the ground and laid it aside. TL handed Wirenut a metal rod. He twisted the end, twirling it open into a clawlike shape. "Let me see the screen."

I held it out for him.

Studying the image, Wirenut carefully inserted the claw,

stopping right at the vial. He twisted the end, and the prongs closed together. "Ready."

David and TL squatted across from each other, gripping a wide plastic tray.

"Not a single speck of dirt can fall on the vial," Wirenut instructed. "If it's disturbed in any way, it'll trigger the toxin."

David and TL nodded their understanding.

"Three. Two. One. Now." Wirenut yanked the claw straight up. TL and David slid the tray beneath it.

I kept my eyes locked on the screen, holding my breath, searching for falling debris.

Nothing.

They moved the tray and claw aside. Down about twelve inches sat the tiny vial with a thin wire sticking out of either end.

Wirenut pulled a slim, red rectangle from his protective suit's pocket. "Something I've been working on. It'll read the timer chip without patching into it. I won't even have to touch the vial."

Good thinking, seeing as how the toxin would release with the slightest disturbance.

"Now's not the time to test a new gadget."

"I know that, sir. I've completed the standard trials."

TL nodded. "Go ahead then."

Wirenut pointed the chip reader at the vial. "Time check."

Everyone looked at their watches.

"Twelve fifty-eight thirty-one."

Little over a minute to go. We all set our watches.

TL stripped sterile plastic off two needles and handed Katarina and Wirenut each one. They each took off a glove and lay belly-down on the grass on opposite sides of the vial. Holding their hands to the side, they pricked their middle fingers and squeezed until blood dripped onto the ground.

Wirenut lifted his eyes to Katarina. "Hey."

Across the small distance, she met his steady gaze.

"We've got this. No problem."

She nodded.

"Twelve fifty-nine fifty," David reported.

Only ten seconds to go.

"Clean." Wirenut and Katarina wiped the blood from their middle fingers.

"Here we go." David tapped his watch. "Five. Four…"

Bringing their fingers over, Wirenut and Katarina held them steady over the opening in the ground and applied pressure with their thumbs.

"Three. Two. Drop."

One single drop welled, hovered, and then fell, landing precisely on the detectors. *Wow*.

Only four more times to go.

"Five. Four . . ."

They cleaned their fingers, held them over the opening, applied pressure.

"Three. Two. Drop."

The blood welled, hovered, fell.

Three more times . . .

Two more times . . .

"Five, four . . ."

Cleaned fingers, held them over opening, applied pressure.

"Last. Time. Drop."

Welled, hovered, and then Katarina sneezed.

15

Everyone froze.

No one breathed.

No one moved.

My eyes stayed pasted to the laptop's X-ray image.

As if in slow motion, I recalled it all. . . .

Katarina's breath hitched twice, and I knew, I *knew* she was about to sneeze. Before I had time to digest that thought, she did. A big one. Possibly the loudest I'd ever heard. No matter how beautiful she was, nothing pretty existed about this sneeze.

But the incredible part? No portion of her body moved. Not even a tiny bit. She kept herself frozen in place as the blood on her middle finger welled and then fell, landing precisely on the vial in sync with Wirenut.

The hematosis detectors fell off and the vial disengaged. Numbly, I watched, suddenly swamped with everything that had transpired. All of it. Not just the sneeze.

Zorba, Rissala, Wirenut, Katarina, Erin, documents, the sword, neurotoxin, Nalani, chains...

The past week of my life smothered my brain in a blur.

The Rayver Security System, jewelry lady, boat, plane, Museum of History, Museum of Modern Art, ceramic egg . . .

I squeezed my eyes shut against the onslaught.

Yellow ribbon, cemetery, marketplace, Gio's guitar, tattoos, water-rigged system, crown, mansion, chimney . . .

"*GiGi?*"

Rental car, necklace, island, diving, marina, pulse bomb, contortion lasers, paralysis cathode . . .

"*GiGi?*"

Cane, green glow, arsenic mouth tape, seizure, blood, TL's blood, my tooth, tool belt, Wirenut's scar . . .

"*GIGI!*"

I jerked alert. "What?"

Everyone stared at me.

David put his hand on my shoulder. "You okay?"

"Umm, yeah."

He smiled. "Good. You spaced out on us there."

"Sorry." I pressed my fingers to the plastic covering my forehead. "My brain's on overdrive. A lot's happened."

Taking my laptop, he clicked it closed. "We all need to relax a little. And to breathe." He unzipped my protective gear. "Get out of that thing."

We all did, greedily taking in the cool night air.

Wirenut swooped Katarina up in a huge hug. "This might be bad timing, but I think we make a great team."

Katarina smiled. "I *know* we do."

Laughing, he twirled her around and around. Their happiness made my heart dance.

He released her and went into his victory shoulder-roll dance. "Go, Wirenut. Go, Wirenut. Go. Go."

I smiled. It seemed like *forever* since I'd seen him do that.

Wirenut pulled Katarina back into his arms. He lowered his head and closed his eyes. She lifted up on tiptoes and their lips met.

And held . . .

And held . . .

They stood wrapped in each other's arms, holding their closed lips together.

The most beautiful, loving, simple, sensuous kiss I'd ever seen. Breathing each other in. Cherishing the other.

Warmth washed over me as I watched them. I should look away, give them privacy. But I couldn't. Their special moment hypnotized me. Mesmerized me.

I wanted that intimacy. That *exact* kiss.

"You all walk back." TL tossed the shovel in the truck. "I'll dispose of the vial."

David picked up our suits and threw them in the truck. "Want me to help?"

"No. Jonathan'll be here soon. I want him to assist me with this."

Wirenut and Katarina pulled back, smiling at each other. He took her hand. "You all ready?"

David placed the tray and claw in the truck. "We're ready."

Wirenut and Katarina strolled off ahead of us, hand in hand, talking. David and I followed.

I stared at their clasped hands, wishing David would take my hand. Why wouldn't he?

Maybe because they're in my pockets?

Oh, yeah.

I took my hands out and stretched my fingers. Sure enough, he wrapped his hand around mine.

A contented smile crept onto my face.

He caressed his thumb along my skin. "You did good."

My entire body hummed in response. "Me? Oh, I didn't do anything. They"—I nodded at the lovebirds—"did it all. Did you see how steady and confident they were? I would've been shaking and rattling like a . . . like a . . . oh, I don't know. Like a something."

"You underestimate yourself. I've seen you in action. You're good."

That comment rolled around in my head for a few seconds. TL had said the same thing. Under pressure, when I *knew* something needed to be done, I did it. Competently. My brain took control of my body's hesitancy. *Well, except for that time in Ushbania when I tripped and split my lip open. And then that time—*

"Stop." David laughed. "You *are* good. Stop trying to disprove it."

"How'd you know what I was thinking?"

He squeezed my hand. "Because I *know* you. I know how that incredible brain of yours works."

Incredible brain. Those two silly words made me all warm and fuzzy on the inside.

I squeezed back. "It's nice to be known." *So nice.*

Wirenut glanced over his shoulder. "What's gonna happen to Erin?"

"Prison."

I moved a little closer to David. "You all right?" I would feel *horrible* if one of my teammates went to jail.

"Yeah, I'm okay." He spared me a brief smile. "TL gave me a letter from my dad. It's the first communication I've had with him since the Ushbanian mission."

"Oh, David, that's wonderful. Is he doing okay?"

"He is. Hopefully, we'll get to see each other soon."

In front of us Wirenut said something to Katarina in Rissalan.

"When'd you learn Rissalan?" I asked.

Wirenut lifted their clasped hands and pressed his lips to Katarina's knuckles. "I picked up a few words while we were on the mission. I don't know much, but I figured I'd better start studying it."

So sweet. I had the best teammate in the whole world. "What'd you just say to her?"

They *both* glanced over their shoulders this time. Katarina's amber eyes held privacy, secrecy, and a hint of mischievousness. Wirenut's? Downright, ornery, none-of-your-business. Neither of them answered my question.

It made me want to know even more.

"What did they say?" I whispered to David. "You know a little Rissalan, don't you?"

"Why are you whispering?" he whispered back.

I narrowed my eyes. He knew why I was whispering.

As we neared the ranch house Wirenut led Katarina off toward the barn. "Catch you all later."

Where ya going? I wanted to tease. *Whatcha gonna do?*

When they were far enough away, I turned to David. "Well? What'd they say?"

He laughed. "When did you become so nosy?"

Gosh, he's right. When *had* I become so nosy? But . . . boy, I wanted to know.

Parrot and Bruiser came out the back door.

Bruiser tossed a football in the air and caught it. "Lookee here. You're alive. Guess everything went okay."

Leave it to Bruiser to be nonchalant about almost dying.

Parrot! I grabbed his arm. "You're the exact person I need to see. Will you translate Rissalan for me?"

David shook his head. "GiGi, GiGi, GiGi."

"What?" I turned back to Parrot. "Well?"

"Now?"

"Yes. Now."

Parrot waved me on. "Okay. Shoot."

"Um . . ." I relayed everything I could remember to the best of my nonlingual ability.

Parrot blinked. "You kidding me? That's not Rissalan. What'd you do, form your own language?"

I punched his arm. "I never claimed to be you."

David opened the back door and gave me a little push inside. "Ignore her. You all have fun."

He grabbed my hand and tugged me down the back hall.

"Where we going?" Suddenly I didn't care anymore what Wirenut said to Katarina.

We crossed through the kitchen, rounded the refrigerator, and David opened the pantry door. He pulled me inside, turned on the dim light, and locked the door behind us.

Gulp.

I'd never been in the pantry before. Small room. Three by five. Lots of shelves and food. What a pantry should look like, I supposed.

What does it matter? I rolled my eyes. *You're locked in here with David, remember?*

I looked at him then, propped against the shelves, arms crossed, staring back at me. His intense dark eyes made my stomach flip.

"Somebody know won't we're in here?" I shook my head. "I mean, won't somebody know we're in here?"

"Maybe. Doesn't matter."

"Oh." *Think of something to say, you idiot.* "Um—"

David pushed off the shelves.

Suddenly, it's very warm in here.

He took a step toward me, and I backed up. Not sure why I backed up. I wasn't afraid or anything.

Well, a little. But scared in a good way. Like excitedly fearful, if that made sense.

David took another step, leaving barely any space between us. I swallowed.

He ran his hand down my jacketed arm. "Hey."

"Hey," I breathed.

David trailed his finger over the top of my hand. "Nervous?"

"N-no." *Okay, it's not warm in here. It's hot. Very hot.*

I reached for my zipper. Wait. *You can't take your jacket off, you imbecile. He'll think you're undressing.*

"No?" He smoothed my hair behind my ear. "I am."

"You are?"

Nodding, David shifted closer, and I swayed back, finding the door solid behind me. Good thing, because his nearness shot my balance.

He stretched his arm above my head, and my heart skipped a beat. "I've been thinking about this a lot."

"This?"

David toyed with the hair on top of my head. "This."

"K-kissing?"

He pressed his body against mine, and I stopped breathing. "Speaking of which."

"I haven't brushed my teeth," I blurted, then realized what an extremely stupid thing that was to say.

His eyes crinkled. "Hmmm, did you brush them this morning?"

"Yes," I croaked.

"Good." He tilted his head.

"Bu—"

David's lips touched mine, and all rambling thoughts poofed

from my brain. His cologne flowed through my senses, buzzing every skin particle on my body.

Soft. Warm. Yum.

If not for his weight holding me up against the door, I would've slid down to my butt.

Cupping my cheek, he slid away from my mouth and over to my neck, nuzzling it. "Better this time?"

Oh, yes. Much better.

Tilting my head, I gave his talented lips and bristly cheek better access. Goose bumps pricked my skin. My breath drained out in a moan.

"GiGi?"

"Hmmm?"

"Is that a yes?"

"Mmm-hmmm." I didn't open my eyes. "Can I have another one?" If not for the turned-on haze fogging my brain, I would've died from asking a question like that.

"Definitely," he murmured.

⠿ ⠿ ⠿

A WEEK LATER. SPECIALISTS Teams One and Two, along with Jonathan and Chapling, packed the conference room.

David and I stood side by side along the wall. I tried to focus on what TL was saying, but my brain wouldn't cooperate.

David.

David. David. David.

Even though inches separated us, his warmth permeated my clothes. I closed my eyes and inhaled.

His scent. *Oh, his scent.*

Nothing like it in the whole world. If I were blindfolded and had to sniff a hundred guys, I'd pick out David in a second.

I opened my eyes. TL was still speaking. I'd find out from Bruiser later what he said.

David shifted, and his shoulder touched mine. On purpose? Accidental? He left it there, barely skimming.

On purpose. I smiled, and warmth crept into my face. I remembered all the kisses we'd shared over the past week.

Did I distract him as much as he distracted me?

He folded his arms, drawing my attention (not that I had any anyway) away from TL. David's muscles stretched the fabric of his long-sleeve T-shirt, molding it to the contours and lines of his arms.

Everyone in the room applauded, and I snapped to attention. Quickly I brought my hands together, clapping, glancing around.

I tried to read expressions, but couldn't figure out what we were celebrating.

"TL recapped the Rissala mission." David nudged me. "You better pay attention. You might get in trouble. I'll have to lock you in the pantry again."

"Shhh," I hushed, although I loved the teasing.

TL lifted his hand for silence. "And now onto the next thing.

With Erin gone, we have an opening in the Specialists. I've asked Katarina Leosi to fill the slot, and she's accepted. She'll be our special-entry operative. Her code name is Cat."

Oh, wow!

TL opened the door, and Katarina stepped inside. She wore a yellow ribbon, the Ghost's signature, around her ponytail. The necklace Wirenut had bought her back in Rissala hung from her neck.

It made my heart all mushy.

Everyone applauded, and I joined in (this time for real). Across the room I caught her eye and waved. Grinning, she waved back. Sitting at the table, Wirenut grinned, too.

So great to see him happy again.

The noise died down, and TL dismissed us. "David and GiGi, I need you to stay."

Huh. Wonder what's up?

Please, not another mission. Pleasepleaseplease, not another mission. I needed time to be me. I wanted to get back to classes. I had to kiss David some more. *Had* to. I wanted to hang out with Bruiser and Katarina and the rest of my friends, my team.

Wait. Maybe TL's going to get onto us for making out in the pantry.

Groan.

TL closed the door, giving the three of us privacy. "Have a seat. There's something you two need to know."

David and I sat beside each other with TL at the head. He

slipped a tiny envelope from his back pocket and laid it on the table.

"I thought it was time to show you this. Open it." He slid it toward us.

David flipped open the unglued envelope and pulled out an old picture. A tiny blond girl stood beside a dark-haired boy a little older. They appeared to be around four to six. Dressed in shorts and T-shirts, they held hands, cheesing it for the camera.

I studied the girl's long hair and blue eyes and then zeroed in on her missing-tooth smile. *Wait a minute . . . what the . . . ?*

I glanced up at David.

Frowning, he stared down at the picture.

I looked back at the boy in the picture and over to David. It couldn't be, could it? "Is this…"

TL folded his hands on top of the table. "Yes. That's a picture of the two of you."

"What?" I gasped. "How?"

"You both lived here and knew each other when you were children. I thought it was time you knew."

I looked up at David and saw his confusion.

I was too numb to understand.

What does this mean exactly?

Somehow, I think I'll find out when TL is ready to tell us the whole story.

Read on for a sneak peek
at the next book in the series:

THE SPECIALISTS
THE WINNING ELEMENT

Prologue

Sisisysy. Sisisysy. Didid yooouuu hear whwhat I aaassskkked youyou?

Sissy pried open her heavy eyelids and focused on the fuzzy image of Ms. Gabrier. Her lips were moving, but Sissy couldn't make out the teacher's words.

Ms. Gabrier stopped talking and stood still.

From across the classroom Sissy squinted, bringing her teacher into focus. She was looking right at Sissy.

Ms. Gabrier's lips started moving again. Her words filtered into Sissy's ears, slowly swirling through her head, echoing off her skull in distorted vowels and syllables.

Sissy dragged her dry tongue around her mouth, trying to moisten it, and smacked her lips. She needed a soda.

Faintly, she heard some giggles, and in her blurry peripheral vision she saw other students laughing at her.

So what? She couldn't care less. Let them and their perfect little selves laugh.

"Sisisysy?"

Dragging her head from the desktop, Sissy slid her butt down. She propped her boots on the desk in front of her and let her eyelids fall back down. Sleep. Beautiful, much needed sleep.

"Sisisysy?"

"What," she grumbled. Couldn't they see she wanted to sleep?

"Priscilla," Ms. Gabrier snapped.

Sissy's eyes shot open. "What?" she snapped back. *Nobody* called her Priscilla.

Her teacher's eyes narrowed. "Do you realize you're failing this class?"

Sissy shrugged. Of course she realized she was failing. She never turned in any homework or studied for tests. Her mom didn't care. No one cared. Sissy's life wasn't going anywhere, anyway. And why did teachers always ask stupid questions they knew you knew the answer to?

"All right." Ms. Gabrier jabbed the OFF button on the overhead projector. "You know what?" She pointed her pen at Sissy. "I've had enough of you. I don't care if you *do* have the highest test scores in the school. I don't want you in here. If you don't care, I don't care. Look around you. Look!" her teacher shouted.

Sissy jumped, took her feet off of the desk, and sat up. She'd never heard her teacher raise her voice.

Ms. Gabrier's jaw tightened. "I said look."

Suddenly very awake, Sissy dragged her gaze over the thirty or so other students in Advanced Chemistry. Mostly preps and nerds. Everyone was college-bound. Some with scholarships, others with daddy's and mommy's money. All of them were staring back at her with mixed expressions. Haughty, disgusted, amused, pity, scared.

Scared of what? Scared of her?

Ms. Gabrier tapped her nail to the podium. "Do you see any of them sleeping through this class?"

Sissy swallowed.

"Do you?"

She barely shook her head.

"That's right. Because they know what an honor, what a *privilege*, it is to be in here." Ms. Gabrier placed her pen on the podium. "There are exactly seventy-one students on the waiting list to be in this junior class. Do you know how many students are on the waiting list to be in this high school?"

Sissy shook her head.

"One thousand eight hundred and twenty-three."

Silence.

She'd had no idea that many kids were on the waiting list.

"You were placed in the Jacksonville Academic Magnet School because of your brilliance. This school made the top-ten list in the nation. Do you know how incredible that is for a public school?" Ms. Gabrier closed the teacher's edition lying on her podium. "What a waste. I'm tired of trying. This is what it's like day in and day out with you . . . when you're here."

Ms. Gabrier pressed her fingertips to her temple. "I'm done. You're out of here." She closed her eyes. "Go fry your brain on drugs in someone else's classroom."

The blond girl beside Sissy snickered.

She turned and snarled back at her. Why did everyone assume Sissy did drugs? She was just tired. Exhausted. Working the night shift at the laundromat would do that to you.

Her teacher punched the projector back on. "Jami, please escort Sissy to the office. And Sissy, take all your stuff. You're not coming back."

THIRTY MINUTES LATER. Sissy climbed in her friend Courtney's open window. She snatched a piece of gum from the pack on the dresser and caught site of her reflection in the dingy mirror.

She looked wasted. No wonder everybody always thought she was.

Heavy black eyeliner smeared her puffy bottom lids. Day-old black lipstick crusted her dry lips. Her dyed black hair stuck out in short, gelled clumps. And the bruise from last week's fight with her mom still colored her chin.

Ms. Gabrier was the only teacher who had asked about the bruise. Sissy had told her she got in a fight with a friend. It was a better excuse than "I ran into a wall." Who actually believed that anyway?

The other teachers had seen the bruise. How could they not? But none had asked. If you asked, then you had to follow up. Paperwork, reporting to authorities, blah, blah, blah. Who had time for all that junk? None of the teachers cared. Or at least none cared when it came to Sissy. Now if it had been cute little Kirstie or peppy athletic Lisa . . .

Whatever. Everyone expected this from Sissy. Bruises, drugs, zeros.